"Now's n... sorry."

For a moment Elizabeth could only stare at Worth, stunned at his interpretation of their kiss. "Right time for what? Kissing out in the middle of nowhere?"

A crooked smile of regret passed fleetingly over his mouth. "You know what I mean. I'm not ready to settle down, to make a long-term commitment, and you're not a woman who'd accept anything less."

Now he'd gone too far. "You're warning me away from you? Are you so conceited you actually think I've fallen in love with you?"

"I'm just making sure we're both clear on where we stand."

His words failed to mollify her. "What makes you think you're so wonderful that when a woman kisses you—" Elizabeth jabbed him in the chest with her finger "—you automatically assume she's after your body or a wedding ring?"

Dear Reader,

Sitting in my red-wallpapered office, I'm surrounded by family photographs. I love seeing my husband as a baby, my father as an adolescent, and my daughter at age four holding her new baby brother.

For better or worse, we all have families. I didn't plan to write about the Lassiter family, but as one character formed in my mind I realized I was dealing with all three Lassiter sisters—Cheyenne, Allie and Greeley. Then their older brother demanded his story be told, and who can say no to a sexy man like Worth Lassiter? What started out as one book had suddenly become four.

I hope you enjoy reading about the Lassiter family and the strong men—and woman!—who match them.

Love,

Jeanne Allan

HOPE VALLEY BRIDES

Four weddings, one Colorado family

One Husband Needed
Jeanne Allan

HOPE VALLEY BRIDES

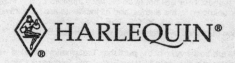

HARLEQUIN®

TORONTO • NEW YORK • LONDON
AMSTERDAM • PARIS • SYDNEY • HAMBURG
STOCKHOLM • ATHENS • TOKYO • MILAN • MADRID
PRAGUE • WARSAW • BUDAPEST • AUCKLAND

For laughing Edith,
with the snow-white hair.

ISBN 0-373-03592-6

ONE HUSBAND NEEDED

First North American Publication 2000.

CHAPTER ONE

MISSION accomplished.

The slow-moving traffic ground to a halt on the road to the Denver International Airport. Sitting in the rented car, Worth Lassiter threw back his head and laughed. On this beautiful June afternoon nothing could disturb his good mood. "Well, Beau," he said out loud, as if his long-dead father could hear him, "you dumped Mom and my sisters on me, told me to take care of them, and I did my best."

He'd married off his three sisters to good, honest men, men he could trust, and in two weeks his mother would become Mrs. Russell Underwood. Russ was a good man who would treat Mary Lassiter the way she deserved to be treated.

A red-tailed hawk soared high overhead. The hawk had lived life more fully than Worth. Traveled more. Had more adventures.

Had more freedom.

Worth thought of the travel magazines stacked in his bedroom, the brochures in his office, and his spirits soared with the hawk.

His grandpa, Yancy Nichols, had taught him a man had to take care of his womenfolk. Worth had been taking care of his for as long as he could remember. For all intents and purposes, the Lassiter kids had been fatherless, supporting each other through thick and thin. Not for one second did Worth begrudge his mother and sisters the years he'd been responsible for their well-being.

Still...

He couldn't stop grinning. The responsibility for his mother and sisters now belonged to other men.

Freeing Worth to do the things he'd longed to do for so many years.

Nobody to tie him down. Responsible for no one's life but his own.

The hawk shrunk to a pin dot and disappeared in the clear blue sky.

No commitments.

Freedom. Adventure. Life with a capital *L*.

Worth could hardly wait to begin.

Flying from Lincoln, Nebraska to Aspen, Colorado with a thirteen-month-old baby wasn't the brightest thing Elizabeth Randall had ever done. She wiped a tear from Jamie's face and said in a soothing voice, "One more plane ride, sweetie, and then we'll be there."

There being a place called the Double Nickel Ranch outside of Aspen. A ranch belonging to a family named Lassiter.

In two weeks, Russ Underwood, Elizabeth's father, would marry the matriarch of the Lassiter family, Mary Lassiter.

Coming to Colorado wasn't easy for her, but Elizabeth couldn't refuse to attend her father's wedding. She knew Russ wanted to introduce her to his future bride and his bride's family.

Russ had told Elizabeth all about the bride's family. About the three perfect daughters who knew all there was to know about ranching and cows and horses. Daughters who were everything Elizabeth would never be. And the perfect son, an absolute paragon, a cowboy to top all cowboys. A man who could do no wrong in Russ's eyes.

Unlike Elizabeth's late husband, who'd rated somewhere below bread mold on Russ Underwood's judgment scale.

The plane taxied up to the gate in Denver. The man sitting in the window seat next to Elizabeth gave her a dirty look and shot past into the crowded airliner aisle. She didn't blame him. The last hour and twenty minutes must have seemed interminable to the man.

Elizabeth didn't blame Jamie either. Her son preferred to approach life at his own speed and on his own terms. The combination of too many strangers, too much noise, too many new experiences, and forced confinement to his mother's lap had overwhelmed her normally sweet-tempered son.

A short walk brought Elizabeth to the gate for the commuter flight to Aspen. With a half hour to spare, she put Jamie on the floor, giving him a brief spell of freedom. He quickly crawled to the nearest row of chairs and pulled himself up on short, stubby legs. Hanging on for dear life, her son made his way down the row of seats, looking back frequently to confirm his mother's presence.

Giving Jamie a reassuring smile, Elizabeth dumped her two carry-on bags on the floor and sat, her back sagging wearily against the chair.

A cowboy moved down the center of the concourse in Elizabeth's direction, his long legs covering ground in a deceptively slow amble. With his wide-brimmed black hat, boots, blue jeans and tan, western-style, sports jacket, he looked as if he'd stepped straight out of a Hollywood western.

For all the man's loose-limbed amble, something about his walk hinted at harnessed strength and controlled power. A shiver ran down Elizabeth's spine as an image from a TV documentary flashed across her mind. A mountain lion on the prowl.

He was one of the sexiest-looking men she'd ever seen. His striking good looks and bone-deep self-assurance attracted the interested gaze of every woman in the vicinity.

An interest he reciprocated, judging by the way he inspected each woman he passed. He caught sight of Elizabeth, and his gaze lingered on her, appraising her.

Butterflies fluttered deep in her stomach, and Elizabeth turned away. She was a single mother, a twenty-nine-year-old widow. Sexy hunks had no place in her life.

After a few minutes, a perverse curiosity compelled her to look for the cowboy. He stood on the other side of the boarding area, his casual stance at odds with the way he scrutinized arriving passengers.

From the corner of her eye, Elizabeth saw Jamie drop to all fours and speed toward a discarded candy wrapper on the floor. "Yuk, nasty. Give to Mama." Down on her knees, she confiscated her son's treasure, making silly faces to distract him. Jamie grabbed her hair with both fists and giggled with delight. Pulling him toward her, Elizabeth hugged his warmth and blew kisses against his silky neck. She loved this perfect little being more than she would have believed possible.

A pair of dark, worn boots walked into her field of vision. "Mrs. Randall?" asked a deep, pleasant voice.

Elizabeth sat back on her heels and looked up. Way up. "Who are you?"

The man unleashed a slow, toe-curling smile. "Worth Lassiter. You are Elizabeth Randall?"

She should have guessed. The perfect Worth Lassiter. Elizabeth looked like something even the cat would refuse to drag in, and he looked as if he'd never had a bad hair day in his life. "How did you know who I am?"

"Russ told me to look for the prettiest woman with the best-looking kid."

Irritation flared at the glib lie. Her father would say no such thing, and if he had, Elizabeth in her rumpled, stained clothes and messy hair hardly fit the description. The man had obviously zeroed in on her red hair.

When she made no response, Worth Lassiter squatted on his heels and held out a big hand to Jamie. "Hey there, partner."

Jamie pressed back against Elizabeth and thrust his thumb in his mouth, his wide eyes staring.

"He doesn't like strangers," she said curtly.

Leaving his hand outstretched a few inches from Jamie, Worth Lassiter casually wiggled his fingers and looked at Elizabeth. "I'd hoped to be here in time to meet your plane from Lincoln, but I got hung up in traffic on Pena Boulevard."

Apprehension prickled unpleasantly at the back of her neck. He could walk and talk as lazily as he wanted, but intuition told her his bright blue eyes would see things she wanted no one seeing. "Why would you meet my plane from Nebraska? I'm flying to Aspen. No one said anything to me about driving there."

"I had business in Denver. I flew up yesterday and took care of it so I can fly back to Aspen with you. You look as if you could use some help. I'll bet this little guy runs his mom ragged.''

Elizabeth's chin rose. She didn't need some candidate for Hollywood pointing out her disheveled state or assuming she was unable to cope with her son. Worth Lassiter wouldn't look so smug and self-assured and—and clean if he'd traveled clear across the state of Nebraska with a cranky baby. ''You needn't have troubled,'' she said stiffly. ''I'm managing just fine on my own.''

The network of squint lines around his eyes deepened. ''You'd think a man with three sisters would know better than to suggest a woman needs a man's help with anything.''

The amusement in his voice scratched against her frayed emotions like fingernails on a chalkboard. She shouldn't have come. It was going to take more strength than she possessed to make it through this visit.

Jamie giggled and lunged for a wiggling finger.

Elizabeth snatched her son and started to stand, but her right leg had gone to sleep, and she staggered, landing in an undignified sprawl flat on her back on the floor. Jamie squealed with delight at the new game, bouncing excitedly on her stomach. People walking by stared down at her. Squeezing her eyes shut in embarrassment, Elizabeth lay on the floor, praying she'd find herself back in Nebraska when she opened them.

So much for the power of her prayers.

''Are you all right?''

One look at Worth Lassiter's face told Elizabeth he could barely keep from laughing as he stood and extended his hand.

Once, she might have laughed with him.

Barely maintaining a fingernail grip on what little composure she still possessed, Elizabeth hung on to Jamie. ''I don't need your help. I don't want your help. Go away.''

Worth Lassiter put both hands in the air and backed up a step. Heat flooded her face, undoubtedly highlighting her every freckle. Setting Jamie on the floor, she struggled to her feet, picked up her son, hoisted her two carry-on bags to her shoulder and walked away.

The plane wasn't ready for boarding.

More passengers had streamed into the boarding area, filling the seats. Without looking at the man steering people away from the sole vacant seat, Elizabeth yanked up her slipping bags and marched over to the row of chairs. "I didn't ask you to save me a seat. I could have stood."

Her ungracious words hung in the air. What was the matter with her? It was as if an evil genie had taken control of her tongue.

Unshed tears stung the insides of her eyelids. A year ago, her emotions had teetered on the edge of hysteria, but for Jamie's sake, she'd pulled herself together after indulging in one good cry. She hadn't cried since. She wouldn't cry now.

Worth Lassiter took off his hat and played peekaboo from behind it with Jamie. Her son leaned forward in anticipation, and each time the cowboy's face appeared, Jamie happily said, "Boo!"

With each "boo" her son crashed backward against her chest. When her flight was finally called, Elizabeth stood with relief, firmly holding a squirming Jamie. "Those are my bags," she said sharply as Worth picked them up.

"Yes, they are," he said calmly, "and I'm carrying them on the plane for you." He walked toward the airline gate.

Leaving Elizabeth with no choice but to follow.

On board the plane, she put Jamie in a seat and grabbed the bags from Worth, silently daring him to object.

Crossing his arms in front of his chest, he lounged in the aisle against a seat back while Elizabeth struggled to put her larger bag into the overhead compartment. Not a hint of impatience crossed his face. She knew darned well he was waiting for her to admit she needed his help. Something deep inside her wouldn't let her. She might not measure up to these perfect Lassiters, but she could darn well handle her own bags.

Gritting her teeth, she finally managed to shove in the bag and settled in the aisle seat with Jamie.

"Excuse me." Worth Lassiter eased past her to the window seat after easily tossing his small bag overhead.

"There are other vacant seats."

He lifted an eyebrow in mocking response to her sharp comment, tipped his hat over his face and leaned back against his seat.

Elizabeth didn't want him sitting beside her. She didn't want him invading her space.

She didn't want to be edgily aware of him.

Jamie let himself be coaxed into taking a bottle, then fell asleep. Elizabeth combed her son's soft, downy hair with her fingers and told herself all she smelled was baby powder.

The subtle scent of masculine, woodsy soap could have come from any of the passengers.

She should have stayed in Nebraska.

She hated ranches. She hated horses.

The forty-minute flight took forever.

Her father was not at the airport to meet her.

Worth watched Elizabeth Randall from across the airport terminal at Aspen's Sardy Field while passengers waited for their luggage. Russ claimed his daughter was completely self-reliant. Never asked for help. Wouldn't need help. But Mary Lassiter had insisted any woman traveling with a baby could use it.

He should have listened to Russ.

Elizabeth Randall wasn't self-reliant; she was bad-tempered, bullheaded, and obnoxiously independent.

Any rational woman traveling with a baby would welcome assistance.

However good his intentions, Elizabeth had obviously interpreted his unfortunate words in Denver as criticism and was determined to prove she could manage on her own. When they'd landed in Aspen, she'd been ready to start a tug-of-war over her carry-on luggage. As if a puny little thing like her could stop him from helping her.

Inside the terminal she'd stuck her pretty little nose in the air, making it clear she objected to his presence so he'd wandered off to greet a few acquaintances.

Darned stubborn woman. Nothing but skin and bones. The smallest breeze would blow her away. She'd refused anything to eat or drink on the plane. The kid was a handful, and her shoulders sagged under the combined weight of him and two bags. The only things holding her up were orneriness and a stubborn, excessive pride.

The afternoon sun shining into the terminal set the disordered strands of her red hair aflame. Hair like hers shouldn't be ruthlessly pinned to the back of her head. It should be free and unrestrained, flying in the wind like the tail of a running horse.

Or spread over a man's pillow.

Which was a heck of a thought to have about Russ's daughter. And a widow to boot.

Compassion replaced his irritation. When a woman's husband had been killed in a car accident the day they'd brought their newborn baby home from the hospital, she was entitled to a little bad temper. Anger was better than the pain and bewilderment he'd caught fleeting glimpses of in the depths of her eyes. Worth sensed that beneath her stubborn independence, Elizabeth Randall was a woman who'd been blindsided by fate and couldn't understand why something so horrible had happened to her.

From across the terminal she glanced at him and hastily looked away when she saw him watching her. Worth leaned against the wall, folded his arms in front of his chest and waited for her luggage to be unloaded. He was in no hurry. Elizabeth Randall wasn't going anywhere without him.

Where had he seen eyes that particular shade of olive green before? Worth swallowed a smile when the answer came to him. Emma Jean, his mother's cat. When something set Emma Jean off, her eyes literally spit anger. A person could tame Emma Jean's bristling fur. He doubted anything would tame Elizabeth Randall's bristles.

A man could lose a limb trying.

She had haunted eyes. Set deep in soot-smudged sockets. She didn't get enough sleep. Didn't eat enough.

The baby wanted down, fussing and kicking. Every part of her body drooped with weariness, but she smiled at her son, cajoling the little boy into better spirits.

She had a beautiful, glowing smile.

A man could forgive a woman almost anything when she smiled like that.

The luggage appeared, but she made no move toward it. Worth straightened and walked toward her, relieved they weren't going to fight yet another battle over her bags.

Elizabeth was watching the terminal doors, her face all lumpy as if she were trying not to cry.

Worth immediately berated his stupidity. She expected her father to meet her. Worth should have made the situation clear. Russ wasn't coming, because Worth was driving her to the ranch.

Elizabeth concentrated on the countryside. She'd never been to Aspen. Hills, green with new grass, climbed from the highway to meet impossibly blue skies.

As blue as Worth Lassiter's eyes.

He slouched lazily behind the wheel of the sport utility vehicle, but he wasn't a careless driver.

Her husband had been an impatient driver, speeding between stoplights, weaving in and out of traffic, jamming on his brakes at the last second, swearing and honking at slower drivers. She'd worried his driving would be the death of them all, but it had been another driver's carelessness which had ended Lawrence's life.

Beside the road a picture-postcard river rushed around rocks and fishermen, tossing glittery spume into the air. They crossed a bridge where a large blue-and-white crested bird sat motionless on a wire over the river. If she opened her mouth to ask what the bird was, who knew what demons she'd set loose? Her entire body ached with tension. A tension heightened with the intolerable discovery that now, of all the stupid, inconvenient times, she was conscious of being a woman. And all too aware of the man across the car.

"Kingfisher." Worth Lassiter had seen the direction of her gaze. "He's been there almost every time I've driven by lately."

Elizabeth knew she ought to respond. Ought to make polite conversation. She groped for something to say.

He spoke first. "Everyone's looking forward to meeting you. They wanted to be at the ranch when you arrived, but Mom said they should let you recover from your flight before they mobbed you. We didn't know you could handle them all with one hand and round up the horses with the other."

Hearing sarcasm in the low, drawling voice, she immediately defended herself. "And I didn't know you were one of those men who feels threatened by a woman who doesn't swoon over your muscles."

After a moment, he asked, "Did I mention I have three sisters?"

"Yes."

"It's like living with three stubborn, wrongheaded mules, but they couldn't provoke me into a fight, and neither can you."

"Why couldn't they?"

He gave her a killer smile. "It was a whole lot more fun making them so darned mad because they couldn't rile me. Cheyenne was the easiest. She'd practically chew the carpet."

"Sibling rivalry. How charming."

"No rivalry. Lassiters stick together," he said in the voice of one stating an obvious, undisputed truth.

Jealousy stabbed at Elizabeth. Maybe if she'd had sisters, a brother, things would have been different.

What would it be like having a brother like Worth Lassiter? She studied him from under lowered lashes. He'd tossed his jacket in the back and rolled up his shirtsleeves. The blue cotton fabric did nothing to disguise the muscled strength of his upper body. Sunlight illuminated light hairs on his tanned lower arms. His big hands were tough and calloused. Like every cowboy she'd ever met, and she'd met a lot of them.

Which made all the more bizarre the disturbing images invading her mind. Not sisterly images, but images she'd never had about other cowboys. Images involving his hands on her body, touching her, loving her while the slow, deep voice drawled endearments in her ear.

Elizabeth squeezed the bag in her lap. Widows didn't lust after a cowboy, no matter how much his masculinity made her nerve endings quiver. Lust was a purely physical reaction which had nothing to do with love and tenderness.

She must be coming down with something. The flu. She should have eaten more on the plane. Gone to bed earlier last night. Since Lawrence's death, she'd had trouble sleeping.

There could be a million reasons why she was having this inexplicable reaction to Worth Lassiter.

The answer came to her. Human contact. Male contact. Worth Lassiter was the first man she'd talked to since her husband had died who wasn't related or trying to sell her something. Jamie had been her excuse for not socializing. The truth was, she couldn't bear encountering Lawrence's friends, hearing their expressions of sympathy.

Couldn't bear wondering which of them knew the unbearable truth.

"Russ worried you wouldn't come for the wedding. I'm glad you did. A man can't get married without his only child being there."

She spoke without thinking. "Russ could."

"You call your father Russ?"

"I assume you disapprove."

"We used to call our father Beau. He didn't like being called Dad."

"Used to?"

"He died some years back."

"I'm sorry." She genuinely was. No one understood better than Elizabeth how devastating the death of another could be. "You must miss him."

He gave her a quick look of sympathy. "It's not like with you. Losing a husband... Russ took it hard."

"I doubt that." Elizabeth dug her fingernails into her bag at Worth's bald-faced lie. "Russ intensely disliked Lawrence and tried everything he could to keep me from marrying him."

Worth's hands tightened on the steering wheel as memories of a conversation he'd had two days ago with Russ flooded back.

The nervous way Russ had stuttered and stammered had convinced Worth that the older man had changed his mind about marrying Worth's mother. Worth had been so relieved he hadn't paid much attention when Russ finally spilled what really bothered him.

His relationship with his daughter Elizabeth.

The scene replayed itself in Worth's mind with total, crystal-clear recall.

"I was real surprised when Elizabeth agreed to come to the wedding," Russ had said.

Worth couldn't imagine why and said so.

Initially, Russ had sidestepped the implied question. "She was such a tiny little thing. If I yelled at her, Elizabeth never cried, but her face would get all funny and her eyes red. I always wanted so much for her. Wished I could give her a perfect world." He kicked a clod of dirt. "It's been over a year since her husband Lawrence died, and she's still mad at me."

Worth gave the older man a quick look from under his hat brim. "Mad about what?"

Russ wouldn't meet his gaze. "The funeral. Our best mare was about to foal. We'd almost lost her the time before, but I told Elizabeth I'd come if she needed me. She said she didn't."

"You didn't go to your son-in-law's funeral?" Worth had to work to keep the disbelief and condemnation out of his voice.

"I knew my ex-wife and her husband would be there. What could I have done they didn't do? I'd just have been in the way. If Elizabeth wanted me there, she would have said so." Russ's defensiveness made plain he didn't need anyone to point out how wrong he'd been. He already knew.

Worth's mother once said men had more trouble than women when it came to dealing with death. She said men wanted to fix things, solve problems. Worth guessed the real reason Russ had avoided his son-in-law's funeral had more to do with Russ hating his inability to make things right for his daughter than putting the needs of a horse before his daughter's needs. "It's not too late to tell your daughter you're sorry you didn't go."

Russ rubbed the back of his neck. "I've tried, but she won't talk about it. She's never said it in so many words, but I know she's convinced I stayed away because I hated Lawrence. I didn't hate him, but he wasn't the man for Elizabeth."

Shoving his hands in his pockets, Russ went on, "There was something about him. Like he was laughing at something the rest of us didn't know. I tried to tell Elizabeth and her mother, but they wouldn't listen." Russ kicked another clod of dirt. "Lawrence was smart as a whip, and polite, too polite. He reminded me of a rogue horse, the kind you don't dare turn your back on. Worried me sick when Elizabeth married him." He uttered a short, bitter curse. "Whatever he was laughing at, he got the last laugh. Because of him, my daughter hates me."

Worth should have given more weight to Russ's comments instead of dismissing them as Russ's guilty conscience talking. Russ was a good man who'd made a mistake. Worth wasn't exactly perfect himself. Wanting life perfect for your family could lead a man into foolishness at times.

Families understood that and forgave the foolishness and loved the thought behind it.

Worth had assumed that if Russ's daughter hated Russ, she wouldn't be coming to the wedding.

Until meeting Elizabeth Randall, it would never have crossed his mind that she might be coming to stop the wedding.

Worth tried to view the situation through her eyes. Her father had disliked her husband, tried to talk her out of marrying him, and had not supported her at her husband's funeral. He knew anger came with grief. Elizabeth Randall needed to blame someone for her husband's death. She'd chosen her father.

Russ's happiness over his upcoming marriage must be unbearable for her, so it must be that she'd come to destroy it. As her happiness had been destroyed.

Worth couldn't let her do it. For her sake, for Russ's sake, for his mother's sake.

For his sake.

After all his years of patiently waiting, no skinny redhead with green cat eyes was going to ruin his plans.

They turned off the highway and crossed the river. Red, clay-like walls rose beside the road before flattening out to rolling ranch land. Colts stood timidly at their mothers' sides. Darling from a distance, but they'd be huge monsters in a year.

In the backseat the bells on Jamie's shoes jingled as he kicked his feet and chattered incomprehensibly.

Elizabeth's hands grew damp. They must be almost there.

Slowing down, Worth Lassiter turned off the road and drove beneath an arched gate made from massive logs. Two wooden circles had been burned into the top cross piece. Elizabeth barely made out the painted words, Hope Valley, on a small sign fastened to the gate. Surprised, she blurted out, "I thought your ranch was called The Double Nickel."

"It is. Named for Jacob and Anna Nichols, my great-great-grandparents. Anna named the area Hope Valley. She and Jacob were newlyweds who moved out west to build their home and their life here, and she was full of hope."

Once Elizabeth had been full of hope.

He parked in front of a large, old-fashioned, two-story white frame house. A porch ran the length of the front of the house, one end shaded by an enormous cottonwood tree. Other buildings were scattered about the area, and a corral near a huge barn held a couple of horses. Further afield a half dozen mares grazed, their spindle-legged colts at their sides.

The ranch reminded Elizabeth of every ranch where she'd visited her father. The barn would be dark and gloomy with snarling, half-wild cats. There would be cows and more horses and dust and smells and noise.

She couldn't stay in the car forever. Worth Lassiter had already gotten out. Elizabeth reached for the door handle.

He beat her to it, opening the door and blocking her way with his body. "Let me give you a little friendly advice, Elizabeth. If you have any issues with Russ, take them up with him, but don't wreck my mother's happiness because of them."

His hat shaded his face, but Elizabeth had no trouble seeing the way his eyes steadily regarded her, almost in warning. A clipped voice had replaced the lazy, dark-honeyed drawl he'd been pouring over her since they'd met in the airport. "What are you talking about?" she asked, confused by the transformation.

He placed his hands on the top of the car, bracing himself as he leaned closer. "You know what I'm talking about, Red. I'm not going to let you hurt my mother. Don't even think about trying to stop this wedding."

Too astonished by his assumption to dispute it immediately, she lost her chance as he straightened and walked away. The situation struck her as excruciatingly humorous. She'd been lusting after his body while he'd been imagining some improbable scenario about her trying to keep Russ from marrying his mother.

Russ walked out on the porch with a blond woman. One of the perfect, horse-loving sisters he'd raved about. Elizabeth plastered a smile on her face and stepped from the car.

Her father walked down the porch steps. "I'll get that luggage, Worth. Hello, Elizabeth, how was your trip?" He stopped a few feet from the car.

"Fine." She widened her smile. "We had good weather."

"That's good." He put his hands in his trousers. "No air pockets or anything."

"No. It was a smooth flight."

"Good. Good." Russ jingled the coins in his trousers. "Nothing worse than air pockets. Always scare the living daylights out of me."

"Everything went smoothly. Sunny skies all the way."

"Oh, for goodness sake, Russ," the woman said, "if you want a weather report, turn on the radio." She ran lightly down the porch stairs and held out her hands. "Welcome to Hope Valley and the Double Nickel, Elizabeth. I'm Mary Lassiter."

"You can't possibly be old enough to be Worth's mother," Elizabeth said in astonishment. Not knowing what else to do, she took the woman's outstretched hands.

"I love her already, Russ," Mary Lassiter said in a laughing voice, squeezing Elizabeth's fingers. "No wonder you think she's wonderful. Now where is Russ's grandson? I can't wait to get my hands on him."

"Here he is." Worth walked around the vehicle, Jamie riding happily in his arms.

Elizabeth's jaw dropped. Jamie never warmed to strangers. As proof, he took one look at Russ and Mary and pressed back against Worth's chest.

Worth rubbed Jamie's back. "Don't worry, buddy, us guys have to stick together. I won't let the women slobber all over you until you're ready to take them on." Holding Jamie easily, Worth gave his mother a quick squeeze with his free arm.

"Really, Worth, I don't slobber." Mary turned laughing blue eyes, so like her son's, on Elizabeth. "I hope when Jamie grows up, he doesn't sass his mother the way my children sass me." She turned toward the house. "I've put you and Jamie in Davy's room, but if you'd rather have separate rooms, we can move the baby bed elsewhere. Come upstairs and I'll show you."

Elizabeth had the feeling of a floodtide sweeping her away. "Jamie," she said quickly and held out her arms.

Worth gave her a long, steady look, then surrendered her son. "I'll get your luggage, while you and my mother have a nice," he emphasized the adjective, "chat."

Dawn popped over the hills to the east in a showy display of golden peach, the morning light stealing into Worth's bedroom as he lay awake. He ought to be up and moving. Early morning was the best part of the day, drinking coffee on the front porch, smelling the wind and hearing the birds twitter awake. The old house creaked and sighed, familiar sounds.

A little voice chattered from down the hall. Worth smiled. Whatever his mother's problems were, the kid was a cute one. Elizabeth was as warm and loving toward her son as she was cool and distant to her father.

Not that Russ had rushed to hug his daughter.

Mary joked her mission in life was to teach Russ how to deal with people as well as he dealt with animals. Worth grinned. At least Russ no longer cringed when Worth's sisters hugged him. As Worth's nephew frequently said, the Lassiter women were huggers.

Elizabeth Randall was not a hugger.

Worth suspected his family had overwhelmed her. Only his niece Hannah, with her red hair and delight at seeing another redhead, had managed to overcome Elizabeth's reserve. He wondered about the funny look on Elizabeth's face when Hannah suggested Jamie's father was probably playing with angels. Playing with angels being Hannah's explanation for the death of her birth mother.

Worth strained to hear, but no female voice answered the baby. During the night Worth had heard the baby fretting and his mother's voice soothing him. Elizabeth had looked exhausted when she'd arrived. She must be getting some much-needed sleep.

His mother hadn't returned to the house. Every night Mary snuck over to the guest cabin where Russ was staying, and every morning she tried to sneak back before Worth arose. She seldom made it, but he always pretended to believe her story about being unable to sleep and taking an early morning walk. He doubted she believed him any more than he believed her, but he had no objection to pretending if it saved her embarrassment. His mother deserved a little naughtiness in her life.

Down the hall Jamie's voice took on strident overtones.

Throwing aside the covers, Worth rose and pulled on his jeans. He knocked softly on Elizabeth's bedroom door, and when no one responded, peeked inside. Jamie greeted him from near the door, bouncing up and down in the baby bed and holding up his hands in a demand to be picked up.

Jamie's mother lay dead to the world, her chest rising and falling in the slow rhythms of sleep. Tiptoeing into the room, Worth lifted the little boy from the bed. Jamie gurgled with pleasure.

Jamie's mother slept on, her red hair spread over the snow-white pillow. Worth felt his body tighten. Elizabeth sighed in her sleep and rolled over, her bottom a rounded hump under the blankets. He didn't even like her, and he wanted to crawl under the covers with her.

Jamie chomped down on Worth's chin.

Out in the hall, Worth closed the door to the bedroom and grinned at the little boy. "You hungry or reading my mind?"

Jamie grinned back, proudly displaying six little teeth.

Elizabeth lay facedown in the bed. A cup of coffee would be heavenly, but she didn't want to disturb Jamie, who was sleeping soundly at last. Poor baby. Yesterday had been too long and too stimulating for him.

And for her. Two of Mary's daughters had come for dinner along with their families. Cheyenne, married to Thomas Steele, had two children, ten-year-old Davy and nine-month-old Virginia. And Allie, married to Zane Peters, with six-year-old Hannah and six-month-old Harmony. The third sister lived in Denver.

The sisters were younger versions of Mary. Both were beautiful and self-assured, their husbands handsome, confident men who clearly adored their wives.

A spasm of envy twisted Elizabeth's stomach. She'd felt like a penniless child outside a candy store, her nose pressed to the window, as she'd observed the teasing family interaction. Children had been passed among the adults with easy familiarity.

Except for Jamie, who would never experience that kind of loving extended family. Her son would never have an uncle like Worth Lassiter.

Worth Lassiter, whose mother and sisters fawned over him. Whose nieces and nephews clearly adored him.

Hannah and Davy had glued themselves to him. Sitting at the dinner table on either side of him. Following him around. Playing with the baby who sat securely and happily on his lap.

Her baby.

Jamie had looked so content—so right—held in a man's large hands. A boy needed a father. Jamie was totally blameless, yet he was the one who would suffer.

Sometimes Elizabeth felt the pain would crush her heart

when she thought of her perfect, innocent baby who'd been born into a situation he didn't deserve.

Sunlight reached the window and flooded the room. Opening one eye, she took in the red cowboy-patterned bedspread and a cowboy boot lamp beside the bed. The room had been decorated for her grandson Davy's visits to the ranch, Mary had explained, giving Elizabeth the room for her stay so Jamie could enjoy the bright colors.

A cow clock beside the bed mooed the hour. Surprised the sound didn't wake Jamie, Elizabeth sat up.

The baby bed was empty.

CHAPTER TWO

"C'MON, Jimbo, open wide. The early bird's supposed to eat all his worms."

"What are you doing with my son?"

Jamie squealed and pounded the tray of the high chair.

Worth turned to face the owner of the furious voice. Sparks practically flew from her red hair. A man would be crazy to want all that heat and voltage centered on him. "I'd say I'm feeding him breakfast, but since the majority of the food is everywhere but in his stomach, you'd probably call me a liar."

"You had no right to come into my bedroom and take Jamie."

So much for gratitude. Worth shoved food in Jamie's mouth and debated apologizing. He didn't debate long. Widow or not, Elizabeth Randall's abrasive attitude was beginning to rile him. Besides, she had no business standing there with sleep-tousled hair, doing bad things to his body. "I knocked, but you were snoring so loud, you didn't hear me."

"I do not snore."

When she stuck her nose in the air and jerked her spine straight, the top of her shiny green pajamas poked out in interesting places. Worth gave her a deliberately obnoxious grin. "You made more racket than a freight train, sleeping with your mouth hanging wide open."

"You watched me sleeping?" She practically shrieked the question.

Turning his back to her, Worth gave Jamie a wink and another spoonful of cereal. "Only for a minute, Red." Revolving to face her, he added in a guileless voice, "I was admiring your green pajamas."

She pokered up indignantly. He could almost feel the elec-

24

tricity as she searched for a response to his compliment which would put him in his place. Worth smiled in anticipation.

"Don't call me Red." His wolfish smile rattled her. His smile and his comment on her pajamas.

She should have taken time to put on a robe instead of panicking when she'd found Jamie missing from his bed. Being in nothing but pajamas and bare feet made a woman feel vulnerable. Elizabeth wanted to run, but instinct told her the dumbest thing she could do was let this man know he unnerved her.

Making her way across the kitchen, she took a mug from the rack and filled it with coffee. She desperately needed caffeine to recharge her brain cells and took a deep gulp of coffee. "Yuk." She spit the mouthful of liquid back into the mug and poured it down the sink. "If I licked tar off the street, it would taste better."

"Does anything around here suit you?" he asked mildly.

"Jamie suits me." She looked at her son and did a double take. "What in the world is he wearing?"

"Since Jimbo and I didn't want to disturb his lazybones of a mom, we had to improvise a little. He was sopping wet."

Jamie gave her a toothy grin and smeared banana on the man's undershirt he wore. "I don't suppose you bothered to change his diapers." Grudgingly, Elizabeth admitted to herself her son didn't seem to be suffering.

"He's wearing a dish-towel diaper with a plastic bag over it, aren't you, Jimbo?"

That made the third time he'd said it. "His name is Jamie," she said tersely.

"Well now, Red," Worth drawled, "Jimbo and I had a little discussion about that, and we decided Jamie is a sissy name. A cowboy needs to have a name like Jimbo."

"He's not a cowboy and he's not going to be a cowboy."

"That's not what his Grandpa Russ says."

"Russ has nothing to say about how I raise my son."

Worth slowly rose. Sticking his hands in his back pockets he silently contemplated her with narrowed eyes. The food splashed down the front of his T-shirt did nothing to subtract from his masculinity. He should have looked ridiculous. He didn't. He looked sexy.

Elizabeth shivered. Only because the house was cool.

Jamie banged on the tray of his chair with his drinking cup.

She moved to step around the obstacle in her path. The obstacle blocked the move with his large body. "I need to take care of my son," Elizabeth said.

"He's fine." Worth studied her face with such intensity the hairs on the back of her neck rose in uneasy protest.

She dropped her eyes to stare at a hunk of banana stuck to his T-shirt. Elizabeth's secrets were her own. She didn't want him, didn't want anyone, gaining access to them. "Please move."

With an exaggerated sweep of his hand, he stepped aside.

Ignoring him, she concentrated on feeding Jamie the last of his cereal, then wet a paper towel and bending down, scrubbed her son's face.

"I surely do love those green pajamas." The soft drawl flowed from the kitchen doorway.

Elizabeth straightened up and spun around so fast she made herself dizzy. Worth Lassiter slouched against the doorjamb, masculine approval filling his eyes with a drowsy, sensual heat. Her stomach zoomed to her toes. She wanted to run and hide. She couldn't move. Her traitorous body reacted as if he were physically touching her. And he knew it.

Elizabeth took a deep breath. "What do you want from me?"

A lazy smile crept across his face. "You know what I want, Red. And I intend to make sure I get it."

What kind of man tried to seduce a woman he barely knew who was a guest in his home? She picked up Jamie, as much to hide behind him as to give herself time to regain her composure. "When you live in a university town, and your husband dies, someone's bound to bring you a book on being a widow. As if it's like learning how to sew or raise puppies. I had nothing better to do, so I read it. The book talked about this."

"This?"

"How some men will tell a widow they know she must miss sex and offer to, well, comfort her." Her voice rose nervously, which both annoyed and mortified her. She forced herself to look him directly in the eye. "Let's get one thing straight, Mr. Lassiter. I am not a lonely widow looking for a man to share my bed."

Surprise flashed deep in his eyes, then he lowered his eyelids to half-mast, concealing any expression. "You know, Red, it's always enlightening to watch a woman's mind at work. I compliment your pajamas, and you immediately conclude I want you out of them."

"If I was wrong, I apologize," she said stiffly.

"A man would be crazy to have sex with you without a fire truck standing by. I don't want sex. I want you to forget the reason you came here, because I intend to make sure you don't get what you want."

"What could you possibly know about what I want?"

"I know you hope to stop the wedding, and I know I'm not going to let you do anything which makes my mother unhappy."

He was so far wrong, she would have laughed. If his exasperating, irrational fixation uttered in a patient, long-suffering voice didn't make her back teeth ache. "I'm not going to stop the wedding," she shouted.

Jamie started crying and clutched at her.

"Good. You don't start any trouble, and we'll all get along just fine." His eyes darkened and a lopsided smile slowly curved one side of his mouth. "Jimbo, you little devil, you." He strolled out of the room.

"Don't cry, sweet pea. It's okay. The mean ol' man has gone." Elizabeth quit grinding her teeth and looked down at her son. And realized Jamie's frantic clutching had unbuttoned half the buttons on her pajamas leaving the top gaping wide open. The cool morning air had hardened the tip of her bared breast to a tight nub.

He was having so much fun watching the color wash across Elizabeth's face each time he managed to catch her eye, they were halfway through dinner before Worth realized the tension at the dinner table could be cut with his dinner knife. Russ and Elizabeth were excruciatingly polite to each other. His mother was trying valiantly to bridge the conversational gap between them. With very little success.

Worth couldn't believe it. He thought they'd reached an agreement this morning that Elizabeth wouldn't cause trouble. Obviously she'd had no intention of honoring that agreement.

Her mistake. He didn't care if her anger at Russ was justified. Nobody messed with his family.

"Elizabeth," Mary said, "your father has told us how much you love to ride. The two of you should check out some of the trails around here."

Elizabeth's head shot up. "I didn't bring clothes for riding."

Worth's senses sharpened. There was nothing about his mom's proposal to cause the hint of panic he picked up in Elizabeth's voice. He didn't like one bit that the panic suggested Elizabeth feared her father.

"It seems a shame not to get in all the riding you can while you're here," Mary said. "If you're worried about Jamie, I'm happy to watch him while you ride."

"That's very kind of you, but Jamie's a little overwhelmed by all the changes in his routine right now. Having me disappear for hours would be too distressing for him."

"You don't want to make a mama's boy of him," Russ said. "He'll be fine with Mary for a couple of hours."

"I haven't ridden for years," Elizabeth said tightly. "I'd get all stiff and sore, which would be no fun with your wedding coming up."

"We don't have to ride that long," her father said. "You gotta be tough to be a cowboy," he added in a hearty, teasing voice.

"So you've told me."

As Elizabeth turned to her son, Worth had the oddest impression that every muscle in her body quivered. The way a horse quivered when terrified. It was clear Elizabeth was adamantly opposed to riding with Russ. Why? What did she fear?

Old family friends had introduced Russ to his mother, but Worth had still checked into Russ's background. He wondered if he'd checked deep enough. Russ's first wife had left him, and Elizabeth and Russ obviously had an uneasy relationship. Russ's surprise at Elizabeth coming to the wedding took on new, ominous overtones.

If Worth had misread Russ's true character in a desire to see his mother happy, now, before the wedding, was the time to find out. Leaning back in his chair, Worth set out to probe into Elizabeth's fear. "Russ, you'll have to drive Elizabeth around and show her the ranch while she's here. You can take your grandson along."

"Jamie likes to ride in cars," Elizabeth said quickly.

"You can see more on horseback," Russ said.

A more perceptive man than Russ would have felt his hair singe at the look Elizabeth gave him. An unbelievably absurd notion began snaking its way into Worth's head. Elizabeth didn't object to going with Russ; she objected to going with Russ on horses.

Russ had boasted of his daughter's riding skills until the entire Lassiter family had grown sick of listening. Worth tried to talk himself out of it, but a gut feeling that Elizabeth was afraid of horses wouldn't go away.

Watching her closely, he tested his hunch. "We raise quarterhorses here on the Double Nickel. Although we've bred our share of reining and cutting champions, most of our horses are good stock animals, trained to work cattle. Too many of them are just standing around right now, eating their heads off and getting frisky. We could bring a couple up to the house for Elizabeth to try out."

"Everyone is busy with wedding preparations," she said immediately. "Please don't bother doing anything special for me."

If she hadn't come out here to sabotage the wedding, he might have admired the way she throttled down her emotions. Emotional women grated on his nerves. With that red hair of hers, he had a feeling those pent-up emotions periodically exploded. When it happened, the fallout must be considerable.

Worth reminded himself Elizabeth's emotions weren't his concern. His mother's happiness was. "It's no trouble at all. I could bring in two or three horses first thing in the morning."

"Put her on Wall Street," Russ said. "That stallion's a lot of horse, but Elizabeth can ride anything with four legs."

For a split second her face turned so pale Worth could almost count the freckles.

"No, I can't," she said sharply. "Ride in the mornings, that is. I spend my mornings with Jamie."

Worth weighed Elizabeth's fear of horses against his mother's future happiness. It was no contest. Life had delivered hard knocks to both women, but Mary Lassiter had never given in to self-pity. His mother had never blamed others for what fate had dealt her, and most assuredly, she'd never coldly planned to sabotage someone else's happiness for her own revengeful purposes.

Elizabeth Randall was not going to interfere in his mother's wedding. Or steal his chance for freedom.

Not if Worth had anything to say about it.

After dinner, Elizabeth went upstairs to put Jamie to bed. In the living room, Worth watched Russ and his mom over the top of the newspaper as they pretended to watch TV.

Russ abruptly stood. "I'm going to bed." He strode out of the room.

Worth waited until he heard the front door shut before quietly asking, "Problems?"

Mary sighed and switched off the TV. "I'm fifty-four years old. I have wonderful children and beautiful grandchildren. Why am I thinking about taking on a husband? Maybe this wedding business isn't such a good idea."

A cold chill went down Worth's back. Elizabeth Randall had spread her poison well if his mother, who deeply loved Russ, was having second thoughts. "What happened?" Worth figured he knew everything but the details.

"It's hard to explain. At lunch Elizabeth was feeding Jamie and she made a teasing remark to him about his daddy not liking beets either, and Russ said he hoped Jamie didn't grow up to be anything like his sissy father. Elizabeth told him she didn't want him to belittle Jamie's father in front of Jamie.''

"That's no reason to get wedding jitters.''

"Russ got defensive and wouldn't stop," Mary said bleakly. "He went on and on criticizing her deceased husband, but as far as I can tell, the only thing Russ had against him was he wasn't a cowboy. Elizabeth grabbed Jamie and walked out of the room. Russ knew he'd gone too far and tried to apologize, but she refused to listen to him.''

Worth pictured the entire episode as clearly as if he'd been there. Elizabeth Randall had manipulated circumstances to make Russ look bad to Mary. The first step in her campaign to sabotage the wedding. "Let them sleep on it. They'll make up." He didn't believe it for a second.

"Her husband's been dead only a little over a year. You can tell by looking at her she's still grieving. I'm wondering if I know Russ as well as I thought I did.''

Hearing the troubled doubts in Mary's voice, Worth gave his mother a reassuring smile. "You've said yourself Russ is better with cows and horses than people. Maybe he's trying to remind Elizabeth that a living son takes precedence over a deceased husband. Doing it badly doesn't mean Russ isn't try-ing to help Elizabeth through her grief.''

"You really think that's it?" she asked hopefully.

"I think he's sitting out in the guest cabin fretting about what kind of father he is and worrying that he's blown the chance to marry the world's most wonderful woman, and he doesn't have a clue how to fix things.''

Mary smiled self-consciously. "Maybe I should go out and give him a few clues.''

"Maybe you should.''

Worth waited a few minutes, grabbed an afghan from the back of the sofa, and sauntered out to the front porch.

Elizabeth sat curled up in the old, double porch swing. Worth handed her the afghan. "It gets chilly here at night.'' He sat beside her.

She scooted as far away from him as the swing permitted. "What do you want?''

"I saw you sneak past the living room while I was talking to my mother. You should have joined us, Red. You might have been able to stop me from repairing the damage you did today."

"Damage I did?" she asked blankly.

"Setting Russ up to look like a jerk."

"He does that all by himself."

"I thought we'd agreed this morning that you aren't going to try and stop the wedding."

"How many times do I have to tell you? I did not come to Colorado to stop Russ from marrying your mother."

"Why did you come?"

"I came because Russ asked me to. Why do you find that so difficult to believe?"

Her claim would be easier to believe if it hadn't taken her so long to come up with it. "You came even though he didn't go to your husband's funeral?"

After a quick startled movement, Elizabeth asked thinly, "Russ told you?"

"He said you're still mad at him."

With slow, painstaking precision, Elizabeth adjusted the afghan, then pulled it tighter around her before saying in a less than credible voice, "I'm not mad at him."

"I can see what a warm and loving relationship you two have."

His sarcastic words hung in the air. Watching some bats swoop down to catch night-flying bugs around the porch light, Worth waited. Familiar night sounds filtered through the night. None loud enough to drown out the sound of Elizabeth breathing or the creaking of the swing chains as he propelled the swing back and forth.

When Elizabeth finally spoke, her voice was strained. "My relationship with Russ is none of your business."

"It wouldn't be, Red, if you hadn't made it my business."

She heaved a loud, long-suffering sigh. It didn't come close to what his sisters could do when they wanted him to know how aggravating they thought him. "If you had half a brain in your head," Elizabeth said, "you'd know I did not come to

Aspen to stop Russ from getting married. Why shouldn't he get married again? My mother is happily remarried. She has been for years. I didn't try and stop her wedding.''

''Maybe you were too young.''

''And maybe you're an idiot.''

''I suppose that's always a possibility.''

''But you doubt it.''

He gave her a slow once-over in the light shining through the living room window. Ordinarily he liked a woman who didn't back down. But not when that woman was intent on revenge. ''I doubt it.''

''It must be nice to be so smug and self-assured. Something you learned at your father's knee?''

''Nope.'' Because he knew it would annoy her, he laid his arm along the back of the swing and gave her a mocking grin.

''Of course not. I'm sure your father was perfect.''

''Beau was a lot of things, but he'd have been the first to admit perfect wasn't one of them.''

''It's hard to believe a man related to you could be humble.''

''Humility has nothing to do with it. Beau was honest. He knew his strengths and weaknesses.''

''Which were?''

''He was a rodeo cowboy with a talent for riding bulls and charming ladies.'' Worth paused. ''And a lousy father and husband. After I was born, Mom stayed here on the ranch and Beau dropped by whenever he needed a place to recuperate after an injury. Once he healed, it was off to the bright lights again, twice leaving Mom pregnant.''

''Don't you mean three times?'' Elizabeth asked,

Worth shook his head. ''Beau picked up women like a dog picks up burrs. Greeley's the result of a fling Beau had with a bartender in Greeley. After the woman gave birth, she drove here straight from the hospital and dumped Greeley off on Mom.''

''Just like that? What did Mary do?''

He heard the horror in her voice and guessed she was thinking of her son. ''Mom raised Greeley,'' he said. ''Loved her. Greeley is one of us. A Lassiter. Lassiters take care of

Lassiters.'' Worth could almost see Elizabeth processing the information as she looked at him, her eyes wide.

''Now I understand. It's called transference or something,'' she said slowly. ''You don't want your mother to remarry, but you're filled with guilt about feeling that way, so you've assigned your negative feelings to me.'' His face must have looked as dumbfounded as he felt, because she continued, ''I suppose you've considered yourself the man of the family for a long time. You don't want another man moving into your territory and taking over from you.''

Worth laughed. ''If you're going to try and confuse the issue with psychobabble, you at least ought to come up with something halfway plausible.''

''I was trying to sympathize with you,'' she snapped.

He gave a disgusted snort. ''Good try, but I'm not so easily fooled. Or sidetracked. Your resentment of Russ sticks out a country mile.''

''I do not resent him,'' she said, glaring at him. ''And I'm not going to sit here and listen to any more of your paranoid accusations.''

He closed his fingers around the clump of hair at the back of her head before she could stand. ''We haven't finished our little chat.''

''I've finished.''

''Then you can listen, but first... I hate your hair skewered to the back of your head like that.''

''I don't care if... What are you doing? Stop that.''

He imprisoned the hand swatting at his hand. ''I've been wanting to do this from the minute I saw you. Here.'' Opening the hand he held, he dropped the hairpins in her palm. ''You don't have to look as if you have one foot in the grave just because your husband died.''

A stark silence met his words before she said in a shaken voice, ''That's a cruel thing to say.''

''It's honest.'' He locked eyes with hers. ''Your husband died, and I'm sorry for what you're suffering, but you have a child to raise. It's time for you to think about what's in his best interests and quit being self-indulgent. How can you take care of your son if you don't take care of yourself? Skipping meals and not getting enough sleep are stupid. They won't bring your husband back to life any more than skinning back your hair will. The man gave you his son. Refusing to live yourself is no way to thank him.''

"You don't know anything."

"I know I'm going to kiss you." He hadn't known it, but now he'd said it out loud, the idea intrigued him.

Elizabeth froze like a deer caught in the headlights.

Worth spread his fingers over her face, his palms cupping her cheeks. Her skin was warm and smooth, like a baby's skin. Nothing about her mouth reminded him of a baby. A full bottom lip wobbled the tiniest bit. Worth hesitated. He didn't force kisses on unwilling women. She didn't back away. Her mouth opened slightly. Inviting him.

He sensed she was as curious as he was.

His fingers slid into her hair. Silky threads snared his knuckles. Slanting his mouth over hers, he kissed her gently, then added some firmness, and when she didn't protest or pull away, he deepened the kiss.

She didn't pull away from him, even if her muted response only hinted at a fiery passion he suspected she'd buried with her husband.

Every muscle in Worth's body tightened, and he knew he shouldn't have kissed her. Because he wanted to keep kissing her. Wanted to take her to bed. Wanted to make love to her until she'd completely freed that passion.

Thoughts of her husband brought back sanity, and Worth lifted his head. The light from the living room fell on her face, and he read a confused vulnerability in her eyes before she looked down. Worth tucked the afghan securely around her legs and curved a hand around the back of her neck. "I'm not going to apologize." Curling a tendril of red hair around his finger, he wondered it didn't sear his skin. "You wanted to kiss me as much as I wanted to kiss you."

"You didn't want to kiss me," she said wearily. "You wanted to intimidate me." Her downcast eyelashes brushed against the dusting of freckles on her cheeks.

He snatched his hand away from her neck. "Are you saying I forced you to kiss me? That you didn't want to kiss me?"

"I'm saying you have this idiotic notion I'm here to stop Russ from marrying your mother, and you'll do anything you can to ensure the wedding goes ahead."

He relaxed. She might shy away from acknowledging she'd returned his kiss, but apparently she was honest enough, at least about that, not to tell outright lies about it. "I didn't realize you were so susceptible to my kisses." Worth swallowed a grin as he felt her stiffen. "That leads to all kinds of possibilities. If I kiss you again, will you shovel out the barn? Repair some fence? I have a whole stack of calving data which needs entering in the computer. How many kisses will that cost me?"

"You rate your kisses too high. If I were trying to interfere with the wedding, which I'm not, you could kiss me from now until the cows come home, and you couldn't stop me."

"Lucky for me that I'm not relying on my kisses to stop you, isn't it?"

"Yes, it—" She stopped abruptly. Several minutes passed before she asked warily, "What does that mean?"

Elizabeth's fear of horses was her own business, and under ordinary circumstances, Worth would never have mentioned it. The possible consequences of Elizabeth's need to punish her father kept this from being an ordinary circumstance.

Drawing a long strand of hair under her chin, he used it to raise her face. "My sisters used to call it blackmail." In spite of her being nothing but a troublemaker, the indignation on her face made him want to kiss her again.

"You can't blackmail me over a silly kiss. I don't care if you tell the entire world you kissed me."

"But you would care if I told Russ you're afraid of horses."

Her sharp intake of air must have sucked in half the mosquito population of Colorado. After a bit, she said, "Me, terrified of horses? That's the silliest thing I've ever heard."

He'd never heard a less believable denial. "You are, and you don't want Russ to know, or you would have told him by now."

She went very still. "I'm not afraid of horses."

"That's good, because Russ is real anxious to put you up on Wall Street. Wally's a good-looking stallion who's all muscle and power, and you don't want to believe the hands if they try and tell you he's a mean, fractious son of a gun." Wally had the temperament of a favorite nanny; even so, Worth never put an insecure or unknown rider on over half a ton of finely-tuned horseflesh.

Elizabeth didn't say anything for the longest time. Then she deliberately pushed aside his hand and stood. "Jamie and I will leave tomorrow." She didn't look at Worth. "I'm not staying where we're not wanted." Her voice was stiff with pride and wounded dignity.

For a second, Worth felt like a heel for harassing her, then he remembered the trouble she'd managed to stir up in only one day and hardened his heart. Catching the afghan still wrapped around her, he pulled her back down to the swing. "You're not going anywhere. Russ and Mom want you here for the wedding, so you're staying. And you're going to behave yourself and forget about your plans for sabotaging the wedding. If you don't," reaching for her hand, he played with her icy fingers, "I'll tell Russ your dirty little secret about being afraid of horses." He wouldn't, no matter the provocation, but she didn't need to know that.

She yanked her hand away from him. "He won't believe you."

"Maybe not. But I'm guessing he'll start wondering when you keep refusing to ride."

"I'm not afraid of horses." She stared straight ahead, her hands clenched in her lap. "I have lots of reasons for not riding."

"I'll bet you made up a real nice list before you got on the plane." It didn't seem to occur to her that if she told Russ the truth, Worth would lose his leverage over her.

"Blackmail and blackmailers are despicable."

"Dregs of the earth," he agreed cheerfully. This time Worth made no effort to stop her when she stood.

"I have my son to think about." She started for the door. "I won't have him hurt by your fun and games."

"Elizabeth." He hadn't run a large ranch for more than his adult life without learning how to crack his voice like a whip. She stopped dead in her tracks. Standing, Worth reached past her shoulder and held the screen door shut. "I would never put Jimbo in harm's way. You can trust me on that."

She turned, leaning against the door, her eyes glittering in the light from the house. "Trust is a word people use too easily. They don't understand what trust is. I have no idea if I can trust you. I don't even know if you know what the word means." Turning back to the door, she removed his hand and went inside.

Worth returned to the swing, contemplating the puzzle Elizabeth presented. Why did she hide her fear of horses from her father? Russ was hardly the type to tell his daughter never to darken his doorstep again, nor was he likely to force her to ride in spite of her fears. A part of the puzzle was missing, which intrigued Worth.

He wondered who'd betrayed her trust.

Russ, because he hadn't gone to her when her husband was killed? If a woman couldn't trust her father, rely on him in her darkest moment, who could she trust? Russ had let his daughter down badly, and he knew it. Worth could do nothing about that. He could make sure their problems didn't hurt his mother.

Elizabeth Randall was a bundle of nerves held together by not much more than sheer grit. A fierceness in her eyes had told him she'd fight desperately for her young son's well-being. She didn't need to fight Worth. He had no intention of harming her or her son, but he would not allow her to compromise his mother's happiness or his freedom.

Her response to his ultimatum had surprised him. She hadn't cried or whined or begged. Or tried to sweet-talk him. He would have believed, had halfway expected, at least one of those.

She could have tried a little feminine persuasion. Tried to bribe him with a kiss or two. Or an invitation to her bed.

He wouldn't have accepted. For many reasons, not the least of which, she was a guest in his house.

He certainly wasn't worried he might enjoy sharing her bed so much that he'd allow her to disrupt his plans. Nothing about Elizabeth Randall worried him. She was nothing more than a skinny, red-haired troublemaker. Worth had handled plenty of trouble in his time. He wasn't worried.

Even if this time, trouble had come with olive green cat eyes.

Elizabeth watched as a chipmunk darted recklessly across the dirt road and disappeared in a patch of wild roses. Dark blue spikes of larkspur waved in the slight breeze. Worth turned onto another road where water trickled along the roadside ditch and willows displayed their catkins. Overhead, swallows dipped and soared in a blue, cloudless sky.

Some might call the landscape beautiful. Elizabeth knew the darker side of nature lurked below the idyllic surface. If a predator didn't get the small animal, automobile tires probably would. Roses had thorns, larkspur poisoned cattle, and the swallows were fighting for nesting territory. In Nebraska, the roots of a willow tree in her yard had caused extensive damage to her house's plumbing.

It wasn't nice. It wasn't pretty. It was life.

Elizabeth knew all about life.

She might not know all about smug, arrogant men who thought they could kiss you one minute and blackmail you the next, but she was learning fast.

A prime example of the species currently sat behind the wheel of a beat-up, dark blue, extended-cab pickup, wearing worn jeans and a faded blue work shirt with rolled-up sleeves. If Worth Lassiter expected her to swoon over the muscles in his forearms, he could think again.

She'd had enough of him and his muscles.

Her mistake had been allowing him to kiss her. All right, kissing him back. For a short time, she'd felt desirable, cherished. More proof of what a horrible judge of character she was. Only a weakling and an idiot would think his arms were a refuge. As she'd learned quickly enough when he'd used her weakness against her.

He'd be positively overjoyed if he discovered exactly how weak she was.

For the second night in a row he'd invaded her dreams. Invaded. Dominated. Starred in.

Dreams of a sexual nature. Dreams she didn't need. Didn't want. He had no right to ruin her nights.

He should be content with ruining her days.

"I came with you today because Jamie loves riding in a car." In the backseat, Jamie gurgled happily to himself. "Your silly threats last night had nothing to do with me accepting your invitation."

No response. As if her claim was so ludicrous, he couldn't be bothered to refute it.

Which naturally increased her irritation. "And I am not afraid of horses. I've been riding horses since I could sit up. I rode my first pony all by myself when I was two."

"So Russ has repeatedly told us. According to him, you're a born cowboy."

"I fell off and broke my arm." She regretted the words the instant they popped out.

He chuckled heartlessly. "Russ forgot to mention that part."

"He usually does."

"Is that why you're afraid of horses?"

"I'm not, and what difference does it make to you if I am? You're like all cowboys. Whether I got an A in math or graduated third in my high school class or did well in college doesn't mean a thing to you. You don't care if I can run a coffee shop or coordinate a convention for three hundred out-of-towners or find rooms for a busload of tourists whose travel agent messed up their plans. Cowboys judge a person by her riding skills or roping skills or cow-chasing skills. Nothing else matters." Belatedly she clamped her mouth shut, having revealed too much.

"Why haven't you ever told Russ you're afraid of horses?"

"I'm not afraid of them, but speaking hypothetically, when exactly was I supposed to tell him?" she asked tartly. "Every summer when I was shipped off to visit him and he threw me on some huge, wild monster who'd been running free all winter and saw no reason to wear a saddle? Before or after the concussion, the sprained ankle, the bruised hip, the horse bite?''

"Those injuries don't sound hypothetical to me."

"Russ has had his share of injuries. You heard him last night. Gotta be tough to be a cowboy." In spite of her efforts, bitterness coated her last words.

"Are you tough?"

As if she'd admit she wasn't. "Doesn't matter. I don't want to be a cowboy."

After a bit Worth said, "Russ can look over a herd of horses or cows and pick up instantly on the least little thing wrong, but I'm guessing he has no clue what makes you tick."

It didn't take a genius IQ to figure that out. "My mother says cowboys refuse to understand any creature with less than four legs."

"I suppose her feelings explain the divorce. I'm surprised she married Russ in the first place."

A question Elizabeth had considered frequently over the years. "Mother was a city girl who fell in love with the cowboy mystique. Ranch life came as a rude shock to her. When I was about three, she had a miscarriage. She needed comfort from Russ, but he buried himself in ranch work, so she cried a lot and they fought a lot and the marriage disintegrated."

"And you blame Russ."

"I don't blame either of them. Onions and ice cream go together better than my parents did. People should marry people they have something in common with."

"Is that what you did? Mom said your husband wasn't a cowboy. What was he?"

"A history professor at the university." She could have added Lawrence was also a liar, a fraud, and a thief, but she didn't. She sensed Worth looking at her.

"I'm not going to bad-mouth him because he chose a different career from the one I have," Worth said.

"Russ does."

"Seeing you hurting must upset Russ. He wants to make

everything better for you, help you cope with your loss, but he has no idea how, so he's angry and frustrated and the only person he can take his anger out on is your husband. It's not logical, but it's human nature.''

"I didn't come with you to listen to a sermon or homespun counseling,'' Elizabeth said tightly. "I'm not hurting and I'm coping just fine with my loss. As you pointed out last night, I have Jamie.''

"And your memories.''

Elizabeth briefly squeezed her eyelids shut against the sharp pain. The last thing she wanted from her marriage was memories. Not after the way Lawrence had tarnished them. Clutching her seat belt she pinned a smile on her face and said, "Yes, of course. My memories.''

Worth paused as he came out of the feed store. Elizabeth crouched in front of the large storefront window pointing out items to Jamie. Her son was trying to gnaw his way through the plate glass.

Grinning, Worth tossed the supplies in the back of the pickup and strolled over to the store window. "I think Jimbo needs a bone to chew on.'' He swung Jamie up into his arms and gave Elizabeth a bland look as she stood. "I would have helped you up, but I know how you hate being helped.''

"I don't need your help. I'd be just fine if you'd leave me alone.''

He felt a curious reluctance to do that. Only a fool stuck his finger in a light socket, but Elizabeth Randall made him want to poke and prod her. Everything from her skinned-back hair to her trim, belted khaki trousers and buttoned-up shirt indicated a woman who believed in controlling all facets of her life. Worth might have believed the outer trappings were it not for the heated emotions which ebbed and flowed deep in her expressive eyes. Elizabeth Randall was made for intense feeling, deep loving and raw passion. He wondered why she went to such lengths to deny her nature.

And knew an insane urge to solve the riddle before she returned to Nebraska.

Securing Jamie in his safety seat, Worth said mildly, "I'll try and remember you want to be left alone."

"While you're remembering that, remember my son's name isn't Jimbo."

"Some things aren't worth the effort of remembering." He slid behind the wheel.

"What is worth the effort?" she asked waspishly.

Worth gave her an amused look, enjoying the sudden color washing across her face.

"Never mind," she said.

"When a woman asks a man a question, it's because she wants it answered."

"You're a real sagebrush philosopher, aren't you? Is there anything you don't consider yourself an expert on?" She strapped herself in.

He turned sideways in the driver's seat, his right arm across the back of the seat and watched her face. "My sisters like to change the subject thinking they can get me off the track. They can't."

"Being single-minded is nothing to brag about. I've never met a man so determined to—"

He cut her off. "Kisses in the dark are worth remembering."

Her mouth closed, and she swallowed hard.

He smiled slowly. "Unbuttoned green pajamas." He had looked away immediately, honorable behavior he had a feeling he'd forever regret. The glimpse had shown him a nicely-shaped, womanly mound. The perfect size to fill a man's hand, its tip hard against his palm.

More red splashed her cheeks, and she swallowed again. "Never mind. I'm not interested in your memory."

Worth lifted an eyebrow. "Then let's talk about yours."

"I have no memory," she snapped. "I'd forgotten all about yesterday morning in the kitchen and Jamie unbuttoning, that is, I hardly remember kissing you because it didn't mean a thing to me, and— What are you doing?" she shrieked as he slid across the seat. "It's broad daylight, and we're sitting in the middle of a parking lot. You can't kiss me here."

He captured her head, his fingers busy with the tight knot

of hair at the back of her neck. ''I hadn't thought about kissing you right now, but if you want me to... My mother taught me it's rude to say no to a lady.''

''I don't want you to kiss me,'' she said breathlessly.

Her eyes were enormous in her pale face, and Worth could read the lie as easily as if she'd written it on a giant green chalkboard. He read other truths there, too. Her awareness of him as a man. Her curiosity. Distrust. And fear.

He wanted to prove she'd lied. Deepen her awareness. Satisfy her curiosity. His gut clenched. Satisfy his. Answer the question as to whether a green-eyed redhead who sparked with anger at the slightest provocation brought that same electricity to bed.

''Your husband was a very lucky man,'' he said.

She stared at him, and then slowly shook her head. ''No,'' she whispered. ''He wasn't.'' A single tear ran down her cheek.

CHAPTER THREE

WORTH could have kicked himself for being an insensitive clod. He'd seen the pain on her face earlier when he'd mentioned her husband. The man had died in a car accident. Where was the luck in that? A woman shouldn't have to endure that kind of suffering.

He wished she'd slugged him or burst into tears. He could have handled those. The single, silent tear unmanned him. Awkwardly he reached over and wiped it away. "He died young, but blessed with a wife and son he loved, he must have died a happy man."

Elizabeth jerked back from his hand. A funny look flashed across her face. "He probably did die happy," she said slowly. The thought had apparently never before occurred to her. It didn't seem to ease her sorrow.

Worth didn't know how to ease that kind of sorrow. The best he could do was divert her thoughts and give her an alternative outlet for her battered emotions. "With luck, he didn't know about your lousy memory."

Her eyes shot to his. He answered the question in them. "You've forgotten I hate your hair skinned back in a bun." This time he didn't hand her the hairpins he removed, but stepped out of the car and tossed them in a nearby garbage can.

"You can't do that." Elizabeth had already fastened her seat belt, and by the time she extricated herself, he was back in the car.

"I just did."

"Stop at a store so I can buy more pins."

"Nope."

"I cannot walk around looking like this."

45

Worth critically scrutinized her. "You're right; it's scrunched together at the back. It needs to hang loose, like this." He combed her hair with his fingers, inhaling the scent of baby shampoo. She must use the same shampoo she used for Jamie. He'd never thought of baby shampoo as a perfume designed to drive men wild. Most perfumes made his nose itch.

She didn't move, a statue carved from ivory. Not ivory. Not with pale freckles sprinkled across her nose and upper cheeks. Not too many freckles. Just enough to draw a man's eye. And tempt his lips.

He trailed a knuckle from one pale dot to another. And watched as faint pink color washed over her cheekbones. His gaze dropped to her mouth. Lips the color of wild roses, they parted slightly, allowing him a peek at a row of perfect pearls. Slowly he slid the back of his hand across the fullness of her lower lip, his muscles taut as he remembered the heat, the moistness of her mouth.

Outside the car, traffic moved and people talked. Car doors slammed, radios blared and a dog barked. Jamie babbled in the backseat.

In the front seat Elizabeth made ragged breathing sounds.

Worth wrapped his hands around her face, feeling the soft, pliable warmth of her cheeks with his calloused fingers. He couldn't look away from her luminous eyes. Emotions swirled across green seas, then slowed, coalescing into pools of sensual awareness.

He wanted to kiss her.

To make love to her.

His body clenched, and he sensed she read his mind as her eyes took on a wary cast. Uncertainty etched tiny lines at the outer corners of her eyes.

Worth's hands tightened involuntarily for a split second before he moved them. She'd been a widow for over a year, but she wasn't ready. Didn't trust him.

Trust him to do what? He wasn't about to start anything with a woman. Not now. Not for years. He wasn't ready to settle down with a wife and family. He didn't want another responsibility. He wanted freedom.

Leaning across her, he flipped down the mirror on her visor. "There. See? You look much better."

"Are you naturally this quiet, or are you annoyed with me for strong-arming you into going shopping with Cheyenne and me?" Mary Lassiter asked.

Elizabeth gave Worth's mother a quick smile. "Worth took me to lunch in Aspen yesterday, but he dragged me past the stores so quickly I barely managed to peek in the windows."

Mary returned the smile. "I hope you're not worried about leaving Jamie. He'll be fine with Russ and Worth."

"I hope so. Russ isn't my idea of a baby-sitter, but Worth seems to have experience with children."

The older woman concentrated on her driving for a few minutes before saying slowly, "Russ wants to be a good father and grandfather. Your father simply doesn't know how. He's afraid to touch Jamie, afraid he'll break."

Elizabeth stiffened. "Is this why you wanted me to come? So you could deliver the second verse of the lecture Worth gave me yesterday?"

"I'm sorry. Was I lecturing? I didn't mean to be." She gave Elizabeth a girlish grin. "My daughters would accuse me of spending too much time with Worth. Growing up, they constantly complained about him lecturing them. Of course, their complaining was all for show. Deep down they appreciated their big brother's loving concern and guidance." Her grin faded. "Having Beau for a father was hard on all my kids, but I think it was hardest on Worth. Beau used to say we must have been inspired when we named him Fort Worth, because there's nobody worthier than Worth."

"Fort Worth?"

"My husband rode bulls and broncos, and we named the kids after places where Beau won big in a rodeo. Fort Worth, Texas, Cheyenne, Wyoming, Alberta, Canada and Greeley, Colorado. A silly conceit, but it was fun. And Beau was right about Worth. He's got more sense of responsibility in his little finger than most people will ever have. From a very young age he felt he had to take care of the rest of us, and he did.''

Mary sighed. ''My dad, Yancy Nichols, died just before Worth graduated from high school, but even before that, we relied too much on Worth. I used to worry he'd crack from the heavy responsibility he assumed. He was always there for me and my girls.''

A reminiscent smile touched her lips. ''Those three girls could get into ticklish situations, but they never looked behind them. They knew Worth would be there, backing them up, literally or figuratively.'' Mary made a deprecating face. ''There's nothing more boring than a mother bragging on about her kids.''

''I'm not bored,'' Elizabeth said truthfully. She wanted to know about Worth. Wanted to know what made him tick. Who better to tell her about him than his mother?

Yesterday Worth had obviously been going to kiss her, but he'd changed his mind. For whatever reason.

She'd been relieved. Certainly not disappointed. She didn't want to kiss him.

Liar. She had wanted to.

And in a public parking lot. Which was insane.

Maybe some day she'd welcome a man's kisses. Not now. Not while the memories of Lawrence's last words festered. She'd given her husband all her love and trust. In turn, he'd betrayed everything their marriage stood for. Elizabeth didn't know if she could ever again trust a man enough to love him.

Not that Worth Lassiter wanted trust or love from her. She wasn't that naive. If he wanted anything, it was a brief fling. Maybe he was the kind who kissed every woman who crossed his path.

Impulsively Elizabeth brought up a topic which she'd been pondering with increasing frequency. ''Worth is very good with his nieces and nephew. And Jamie.'' Usually when someone picked up Jamie, worry gripped her. Even her stepfather, whom she adored, made her nervous when he held her son.

Yet she trusted Worth with Jamie. Because she knew with complete certainty, without knowing how she knew, that Worth would never hurt a child. "I'm surprised he hasn't married and started his own family."

"Not for lack of opportunity. I swear, since Worth turned ten, we've had females hanging around the ranch, each hoping he'd fall madly in love with her. He has his share of women friends, but nothing serious." Mary sighed. "Sometimes I wonder if having assumed responsibility for his sisters from such a young age, Worth feels as if he's already raised his family."

Her voice lightened. "His sisters say he's so spoiled by having hordes of women at his beck and call, he can't bear to give them all up and settle for just one."

His mother's comments put Worth's kisses in their proper perspective. He obviously dispensed meaningless kisses as cavalierly as other people dispensed smiles. Worth was probably constitutionally unable to pass an unattached woman without kissing her. For all Elizabeth knew, he kissed every attached woman who came on his horizon, as well.

Not that she cared whom he kissed. Those weren't pangs of disappointment or jealousy she felt. Hunger pangs, for lunch. That was all they were.

"I'm sure he'll quit playing around and find the right woman some day," Elizabeth said to his mother, before asking about their surroundings.

Mary pointed out Mt. Sopris and the Roaring Fork River. The rest of the way into Aspen their conversation was that of tour guide and visitor.

Worth gave a low whistle as his mother descended the staircase. "Hey, beautiful lady, where did you come from?"

"You think this dress is okay? I mean, I bought a dress last week for the party, but this morning it looked like an old lady's dress, and while I'm old, darn it, I want to look good for Russ, and Cheyenne insisted this dress is perfect."

He swung his mother off the bottom step. "You look fantastic. Russ will have to spend the evening fighting off all the bachelors who want to trade places with him.''

A knock sounded at the door. Mary smiled nervously at Worth and went to greet Russ. Worth almost laughed out loud at the dead silence which followed the opening of the door. Russ might have seen Mary in something other than jeans, but Worth doubted he'd seen her wearing a drop-dead gorgeous dress like the short, white, beaded number she wore now. Mary Lassiter had darned good legs, even if she was his mother and fifty-four years old.

The older couple went out on the porch, further amusing Worth. The two behaved like a couple of teenagers. He ought to flash the porch lights as he used to do when his sisters came home from dates and lingered too long out there.

Jamie's voice babbled from upstairs, and footsteps descended behind Worth. He turned. After a minute he managed to wrestle his jaw back into place, but he couldn't do a thing about the rest of his body's response to the woman coming down the stairs.

"Give me Jimbo and the diaper bag." He cleared his throat. "He'll mess up your dress."

On second thought, he ought to leave the kid in her arms. Maybe Jamie would throw up on it and she'd have to change. Into something decent.

So much for grieving widows.

She handed over her son and bag. "Your sister Cheyenne is rather overwhelming, isn't she?" Elizabeth asked, not meeting Worth's eye. "I brought with me a dress I used to wear to faculty dinners and it was perfectly fine but your mother insisted Russ wanted to buy me a dress and I found a nice plain gray one but Cheyenne wouldn't let me buy it and this one's too glamorous for me, isn't it? You're not saying anything. I knew I shouldn't have let her talk me into it. It's not me and I feel like a fool. I look like one, don't I?"

She didn't look like a fool. Worth patted Jamie's back, forced a smile to his face, and tried to come up with a convincing argument to persuade her to change into something that wouldn't have every man at the party panting after her.

"Obviously I look so ridiculous, you can't think of anything nice to say. It will take me only a minute to change." Elizabeth whirled around and started back up the stairs. She didn't turn in time to hide the hurt look on her face.

"No, don't change. You don't look ridiculous." She looked so sexy his body temperature must have risen fifty degrees. He scrambled for an explanation of his silence. "I was being amused by the fact that not five seconds ago my mother came down all worried about her dress. You both look great."

Elizabeth turned, hovering on the staircase. "You don't think the dress is too, well, sexy?"

Worth swallowed the answer he wanted to shout and made an effort to study the dress objectively. Orange and tomato-red flowers cascaded down shiny material the color of a ripe Colorado peach. She shimmered as light hit the material. Thin straps held up the dress which stopped short of her knees and fit her curves like a glove. She might be thin, but her figure was definitely a woman's.

He knew he'd seen ten times more skin exposed on other women in Aspen, but he'd never felt a compulsion to cover up those women with Jamie's baby blanket. He didn't like the feeling. "The dress is fine," he said, not meaning a word of it.

"You're sure?"

"Did my mother like the dress?" At Elizabeth's nod, he said, "That settles it, then. Mom and Cheyenne wouldn't persuade you to wear something inappropriate." He was going to strangle Cheyenne when he saw her. This close to her wedding, his mother could be excused for fuzzy thinking, but Cheyenne? So much for the notion that his brother-in-love could control his wife.

"You're really sure I look okay?"

He clamped his molars together and nodded.

The front door opened behind him. "You sure look nice, Elizabeth. She's pretty as a picture, isn't she, Mary?"

Worth turned to stare in disbelief at Russ's proud, beaming countenance. Was the man blind? His daughter didn't look nice. She looked like a luscious, sexy peach. Ripe to be picked.

Cheyenne and Thomas Steele's home was large, tastefully decorated and warm with personal touches. Acres of marble surrounded exquisite Oriental rugs, and huge glass windows framed breathtaking views of Aspen and the surrounding countryside. Important pieces of art hung in some rooms, while other rooms showcased enlarged black and white historical photos of Aspen and Colorado. The small breakfast room featured framed artwork created by the Steeles' son Davy and his cousin Hannah Peters.

Allie and Zane Peters were here, along with the third sister, Greeley, who'd come from Denver with her husband, Quint Damian. Once again Elizabeth was struck by the bonds between the various families. More than relatives, Worth and his sisters and their spouses were close friends.

Elizabeth envied them, and envied the way the children moved easily among them. Periodically Hannah and Davy trotted down from the upstairs sitting room where Cheyenne's nanny watched the children. Hannah would give Elizabeth a report on Jamie while Davy unconsciously aped Worth's way of standing and talking as he discussed horses and tractors with his uncle.

Cheyenne had gathered a fascinating mix of guests to honor the bridal couple. Elizabeth recognized many faces from the newspapers. Political figures, movie and TV stars. She supposed others were local movers and shakers. When pushed, Worth had pointed out ranchers and longtime friends of the Lassiters, as well as friends and schoolmates of the younger generation of Lassiters.

He'd introduced her to none of them.

Elizabeth accepted the glass of wine Worth handed her and thanked him. He replied in the same tight-lipped tone of voice he'd been using all evening. The way he cordoned her off from everyone, she felt as if she had rabies. "You don't have to spend the evening standing guard,'' she said sharply. ''I'm not planning to cause trouble between Mary and Russ, so quit fussing about it.''

Worth gave her an odd look. ''I never fuss, and I'm not worried about you causing trouble tonight between Russ and Mom.'' He didn't move from her side.

Elizabeth tapped her foot in growing irritation. ''Why aren't you worried? Because you think your stupid threat to blackmail me scares me? It doesn't.''

He just shrugged and drank his wine.

A different horrible suspicion grew on her. ''It's because your mother ordered you to take care of me, didn't she? I don't need you to take care of me. Go make one of your thousands of girlfriends happy. I'm going to the ladies' room.''

She heard Worth choking on his wine as she walked away.

Greeley was headed in the same direction as Elizabeth. As they met, Greeley glanced toward her brother and made a face. ''When Mom marries Russ, you'll be part of the family, Elizabeth, and you're going to have to be a lot tougher, or Worth will walk all over you. I don't know what he's told you, probably all lies, but don't let him get away with it.''

Joining them, Cheyenne caught the look on Elizabeth's face. ''Greeley's teasing you. Worth has never told a lie in his life. All the same, right now, I'm furious with him, the way he's acting.''

''I told you you'd never fool Worth,'' Greeley said. ''Can you come up with one time any of us managed to outmaneuver him?''

''I don't know how he found out I invited three women to meet him, but he obviously thinks he's outsmarted me by gluing himself to you,'' Cheyenne said, addressing Elizabeth.

Only slightly enlightened, Elizabeth felt her way. ''You invited some women to meet Worth?''

''We've run out of possibilities around here, so I invited a friend from Denver, and a couple of women I really like who work for Thomas, one from New York and one from Charleston. They're all terrific, but will Worth bother to give any of them the time of day? Naturally not. At least I didn't tell them what I had in mind.''

"You're matchmaking?"

"Russ and Mom plan to enlarge the guest house, and Worth will be all alone in that big old house," Greeley said. "He's taken care of us all these years. Now it's our turn to take care of him.''

"We want him to be as happy as we are. Worth being Worth, he can't admit his little sisters know anything, so he's fighting us all the way." Cheyenne scowled across the room. "Just look at him standing there discussing who knows what with men instead of giving the women a chance."

"He's not exactly ugly. Why can't he find his own girl-friend?"

"He's too well-mannered for his own good," Greeley explained.

Cheyenne added, "He smiles and he's polite and he listens and women fall in love with him. He tries to discourage them, but he can't bring himself to be rude, so the women convince themselves he's in love with them. He hates to hurt their feel-ings so it's easiest for him to stay totally detached. He'll never meet the right woman that way."

"He can't bring himself to be rude?" Elizabeth repeated in disbelief. She'd never met anyone so rude.

"Well, he has no problem telling us what's what," Chey-enne qualified, "but we're his sisters. Growing up, he was always on our case about doing the right thing and about our responsibilities, and on and on and on. A person would think we were juvenile delinquents the way he lectured us. And he's so devious. We'd swear we weren't going to do something he thought we ought to do, and before we knew how it happened, there we were doing it. Worth always thinks because he's the oldest, he knows what's best for us."

"He's rude to me and I'm not his sister."

"Your father is marrying our mother." Greeley laughed wryly. "Welcome to the family. And the first rule is, don't ever let Worth have the upper hand. He's the best brother in the world, but you don't ever want to let him manipulate you for his own insufferable purposes.''

''As he is now,'' Cheyenne said, turning her scowl on Elizabeth. ''Every woman here thinks you're Worth's girlfriend, thanks to the way he's behaving.''

''I'm not...he's not...'' Elizabeth sputtered in her haste to deny any relationship whatsoever between her and Worth.

''Of course not,'' Cheyenne said impatiently. ''Worth wants me to mind my own business, so he's using you to keep other women away.''

Elizabeth couldn't care less whether Worth found a wife, loving or otherwise. What she did care about was being used. She knew exactly how to turn his manipulating tricks back on him. ''Point out your three friends.''

When Elizabeth rejoined the party, Worth was waiting for her. ''Mom did not order me to do anything,'' he said without preamble, ''but you are a guest of our family. The party is in Mom's and Russ's honor, and Cheyenne has hostess duties, so I'm taking care of you, as they would if they weren't busy. I simply want to make sure you're having a good time.''

Elizabeth gave him a long look, his sisters' words echoing in her head. He had a real gift for manipulation. Not only was he using her, he pretended he was doing it for her own good. Next he'd demand gratitude. She reined in her irritation and smiled determinedly. ''That's very kind of you. Isn't that Jake Norton, the movie star over there? I'd really like to meet him.'' The actor was talking to Cheyenne's single friend from Denver. ''He looks as handsome in real life as he does in the movies. I always figured make-up and camera angles made all the difference,'' she widened her eyes, ''but he's drop-dead gorgeous.''

''He's married.''

''I'm not going to elope with him. I just want to meet him.''

Worth muttered something unintelligible in his wine.

Elizabeth turned down the corners of her mouth. ''I suppose you don't want to introduce me because you're worried I'll embarrass you by doing something tacky like asking for his autograph.''

Taking hold of her elbow, Worth practically hauled her across the room to the actor's side where the two men exchanged good-natured insults before Worth introduced Elizabeth as Russ's daughter.

Jake Norton introduced the woman with him and smiled his famous heart-stopping smile. The one which caused females from four to one hundred and four to fall madly in love with him. Elizabeth's heart didn't miss a beat. She was immune to falling in love, madly or otherwise.

Apparently the woman from Denver was also immune to the actor's smile, judging by the unattractive way she drooled at Worth during introductions. Worth would never be interested in someone so obvious.

A petite brunette dashed up, threw her arms around Worth's neck and noisily kissed him. Jake Norton rolled his eyeballs and said, "My wife, Kristy."

Kristy Norton emerged from Worth's embrace and laughed.

Not that Elizabeth was jealous, but she saw absolutely no reason the actor's wife had to cling to Worth while her husband made introductions all around.

Casing the room, Elizabeth spotted Thomas Steele talking to the woman from New York. "I haven't had a chance to say anything other than hello to your brother-in-law." She excused herself to the Nortons and Ms. Denver.

Worth trailed her like a puppy on a leash. Ms. New York couldn't keep her eyes off Worth as he chatted with Thomas. Smitten, but inhibited by good manners, Elizabeth decided. Rudely she cut into the men's conversation. "I didn't realize you were the Steele in Steele hotels, Thomas. I'm in hotel management myself." She named the exclusive chain where she'd worked her way up from night clerk before taking an extended maternity leave. Turning to the woman, Elizabeth asked what she did, drawing her into a discussion with Thomas of the hotel business. The woman was bright, articulate and funny.

Also a very chic urbanite. Not at all Worth's type.

Elizabeth looked around the room for the woman from Charleston. She spotted her in the next room standing in front of a huge framed watercolor of a man and a horse. A cowboy. "You have some of the most gorgeous artwork on your walls, Thomas. I have to get a closer look at that watercolor." She took off, confident her shadow would stick with her.

The southern woman was raven-haired, intelligent, droll, and gorgeous. She was fascinated by cowboys and the Old West and had been riding horses since she was three. She eyed Worth with the same longing a thirsty Jamie showed for a cup of juice.

Elizabeth knew without a doubt the woman's "ya'alls" and slow-talking, syrupy accent would drive Worth insane.

Worth laid a heavy arm over Elizabeth's shoulders. "If you'll excuse us, Elizabeth and I haven't checked out the buffet yet, and I know she's starving." Before they'd gone two feet, he murmured in her ear, "Finished now, Red, or are there more than the three Thomas told me about?"

Elizabeth stopped, digging her high heels into the Oriental rug. "Cheyenne was right. You did know."

"I knew about the women. The part I'm not clear about, is how my sister roped you into her scheme."

"She didn't. You did."

"Me?" Worth didn't think he could have heard right. She was glaring at him as if he were the instigator of his sister's plot instead of its victim.

"You were using me." She stuck her nose in the air and walked away, her spine rigid with indignation.

As much as he enjoyed the sight of her irate hips snapping across the room, Worth intended to find out exactly what was going on. He strode after her. Thomas and Cheyenne must have invited every disreputable man in a tristate area, and too many of them thought they heard a redheaded siren's call. If he had one more so-called friend beg for an introduction... Catching up with Elizabeth, Worth put his hand against the middle of her back and steered her toward the French doors leading to the outside courtyard.

Barely noticing the strings of tiny electric lights outlining the stone outer walls and the garden paths, he marched her toward a round table in the far corner.

"Stop," Elizabeth said suddenly. "Is this one of Greeley's?"

"Yes." They stood in front of the floodlit sculpture his youngest sister had created for Cheyenne's family.

"Russ told me about her sculptures, but I had no idea..." Elizabeth's voice faded away as she read the small metal plate at the base of the sculpture. "Kinds of Love." She walked slowly around it, studying the twisted hunks of metal. "The hearts are obvious, but this is hardly a cliché. So much raw emotion. Look how one section flows into another, as if the love is growing and joining... Explain the sculpture to me."

"It's Greeley's tribute to those who are loving and generous enough to open their hearts to a needy child."

"Love growing and encompassing..." Elizabeth reached out and gently glided a finger over a reformed bumper. "No wonder it's so powerful." She hesitated. "It's not an easy thing, loving a child not your own."

Worth led her to the corner table. Heat from the outdoor gas fireplace didn't quite reach them, and when she shivered, he removed his jacket and placed it over her shoulders.

She thanked him with a smile and held the jacket close around her. "I'm not really cold. Greeley's sculpture sent shivers down my spine."

More strings of electric lights wrapped the spines of the umbrellas over the tables. Elizabeth's face glowed in the soft light.

"Greeley isn't the only one loved by someone other than her natural parent." Worth had seen the effect of the sculpture on Elizabeth and reached his own conclusions.

"No." She gave him a quick smile. "Dad, John Randall, my stepfather, married Mother when I was six."

Worth considered the wealth of information in those few

words. She called her stepfather Dad, and her real father Russ. Her voice was warm and loving when she spoke of John Randall. Randall was her last name. Worth doubted it was a coincidence. "You and your stepfather have the same last name?"

"Yes." An odd look flashed across her face. "Russ didn't tell you I married my stepfather's son? Mom thinks that's why Russ disliked Lawrence so much. A subconscious thing because he resents her marrying John and being so happy with him."

"Do you agree with your mother?" Worth had found Russ a pretty good judge of a man's character and wondered at Elizabeth's mother readily dismissing her ex-husband's concerns.

"No. I've always thought Russ felt badly their marriage didn't work out, but I'm sure he wished her well with Dad and was glad she was happy." She added flatly, "Russ didn't like Lawrence because he wasn't a cowboy."

No matter how many times he heard it repeated, Worth rejected the notion that Russ disliked Elizabeth's husband for that reason. Nothing in Worth's investigation of Russ even hinted at Russ being small-minded. Worth turned the conversation back to Elizabeth's stepfather. "You like this John Randall a lot?"

She nodded. "He's been very good to me."

He pictured a skinny, freckled little girl, all knees and elbows, with flyaway red hair. "I'll bet he spoiled you rotten."

"I was a model child," she said primly before her mouth curved upward.

"Did your stepbrother—Lawrence—live with you?"

Her smile vanished. "No. I thought you were hungry. Why did you drag me out here where there's no food?" Her eyes narrowed. "Never mind. I can figure it out. I suppose everyone is supposed to think we're out here kissing or something. That is so juvenile."

Puzzled by her abrupt change of subject, the rest of her conversation didn't sink in at first. When it did, it made no sense. ''Kissing is juvenile?'' There was nothing juvenile about kissing her. Unless one considered playing with dynamite a juvenile pastime.

''I know all about the so-called perils of your bachelorhood. I know what a burden it must be for you,'' sarcasm coated her words, ''to have women chasing after you and falling in love with you.''

Sisters, Worth thought in disgust. He couldn't be plagued with easy things like locusts or hailstones or a bad back. No, he got landed with three sisters. ''If this is about Cheyenne playing matchmaker again, I've told her time and time again I no longer feel obliged to entertain or encourage any of these single women she feels compelled to drag past me. I'm not some stallion standing at stud.''

Elizabeth's eyes widened at the coarse comparison, but she merely said, ''I don't care if you resent your sisters trying to help you, but I will not be used.''

''Cheyenne claims she's trying to help me?'' Worth asked incredulously before Elizabeth's last words resonated. ''What do you mean, use you? That's the second time you've accused me of using you.''

''You admit you knew Cheyenne had invited three friends to meet you. You're not interested so you've been pretending all evening that you're interested in me.'' She filled the last word with outrage. ''You want everyone to think we have something going so they'll think you're unavailable. Forget it.'' Standing, she thrust his jacket at him and headed back toward the house.

Her conclusion was so far from the truth, Worth couldn't help laughing as he followed her. He'd been protecting the merry widow from unwanted advances, and she thought he'd been using her to escape his sister's matchmaking scheme. So much for doing a good deed.

The plan came from nowhere. Liking it, he examined it carefully as he eyed the shapely form speeding off in a huff ahead of him.

She was an unknown quantity which meant the plan could

be dangerous, but the reward justified the risk. And not that big a risk. Too much was at stake for him to be tempted. He wasn't about to trade his much-anticipated freedom for red hair spread across his pillowcase. When he was ready to settle down, there would be other women who physically attracted him.

"I don't like that look on your face," she said uneasily as he beat her to the door and ushered her inside.

His doubts vanished. Elizabeth Randall might be a widow, but she was too naive to take advantage of his plan. Worth gave her his best, innocent, boyish, kindly uncle, friendly, brotherly, persuasive grin. If his sisters had seen him, they would have yelled at her to run for cover. His sisters were nowhere in sight. "I think the best thing you and I can do is come to a mutual arrangement."

"What kind of mutual arrangement?" she asked warily.

"Elizabeth? Elizabeth Randall?"

Worth turned as a smooth, baritone voice spoke behind him. With a single glance, he took in the white, pseudo-pirate, silk shirt and snug black trousers. The middle-aged man, a stranger to Worth, had actor written all over him.

Brushing past Worth, the man dipped his head toward Elizabeth and took her unresisting hand. "I thought it was you, my dear, but then I saw the dress and doubted my eyes, but it is you, isn't it? There's no need to ask how you're doing, when it's obvious you're blooming. You look radiant, my dear, positively radiant."

Worth wanted to plant his fist right smack in the middle of the man's smarmy face.

CHAPTER FOUR

RETRIEVING her hand with some difficulty, Elizabeth managed a polite smile. "Professor Burns. What a surprise to see you here."

He gave her an arch look. "The surprise is seeing you here, my dear. You've been quite reclusive since Lawrence's death."

She hated the way his eyes kept straying to her chest. "My father is marrying Mrs. Steele's mother, Mary Lassiter. This party is for them."

"Oh yes. I seem to remember Lawrence saying something about your father being a cowboy." He faintly sneered the last word.

Elizabeth reminded herself she'd known the professor for over two years without kicking him in the shin. Now wasn't the time to start. "Are you a friend of Mary Lassiter's?"

"I'm visiting friends in Aspen, and my host and hostess asked the Steeles if they might bring me along. Hardly a concession on the Steeles' part, based on some of the people I've met thus far. The Steeles appear to be extremely democratic in their guest list. I understand Steele is wealthy, so perhaps the guests reflect Mrs. Steele's having married well."

Elizabeth couldn't help stealing a quick look at Worth. His eyes narrowed slightly at the slur toward his sister, but the pleasant expression on his face never wavered. Somehow she didn't feel much reassured. "Professor Burns—"

"Augustine," he interjected smoothly. "My dear, I must insist you use my first name. We've been friends for a long time." He gave her a look which seemed to suggest if they hadn't been very good friends before, it was time they became so.

62

Ignoring her churning stomach, Elizabeth smiled vaguely and continued, "I'd like to introduce Mrs. Steele's brother, Worth Lassiter. Worth, this is Augustine Burns. From the university where Lawrence taught."

Worth reached out and grabbed Professor Burns' hand and pumped it vigorously. "Howdie. Right nice to meet cha, Gus."

Elizabeth almost swallowed her tonsils at Worth's broad twang. The men continued to shake hands, each obviously indulging in a macho endeavor to out-muscle the other. The professor's neck bulged.

Worth finally released him. "Goldarn, I'm tickled pink to meet a teaching buddy of Larry's. So, whaddya teach, Gus?"

If Professor Burns—Gus—stiffened much more, his spine would shatter. Elizabeth swallowed the nervous bubble of laughter rising in her throat and stared at a crystal chandelier at the end of the room.

"I'm a professor of history," he intoned in an arctic voice.

"Way ta go, Gus. I'll bet them pupils of yours are right happy when they got you up in front of the blackboard." Worth slapped him on the back.

Augustine rocked forward on his toes. Elizabeth almost felt sorry for him.

"How do you make your living, Mr. Lassiter?"

"If ya seen what's on the bottom of my boots, you wuddn't haf to ask." Worth made an alarming hee-hawing noise through his nose.

Elizabeth assumed he was supposed to be laughing. Almost reluctantly she decided to put an end to his outrageous behavior. "Nice to see you, Augustine," she said politely, if untruthfully. "I hope you enjoy your stay in Aspen."

"Now that I know you're here, my dear," he gave her a heavy-lidded look which came off more ludicrous than sensual, "and have cast off your widow's weeds, shall we say? I—"

"Let's don't say," Worth said evenly.

Augustine stared at him. "I beg your pardon?"

"Elizabeth came to Aspen for her father's wedding. She isn't your dear, and she doesn't have time to fend off unwanted advances from a pretentious, aging psuedo-intellectual with pubescent manners and uncontrolled hormones,'' Worth said in a level voice. ''Elizabeth, I believe we were on our way to the buffet table. If you'll excuse us, Gus, I seem to have worked up quite an appetite.''

Waiting until they had moved beyond range of Professor Burns' hearing, Elizabeth gave Worth a dry look. ''Shouldn't you be hungrier than a hog with something or other?''

Amusement lit his eyes. ''I believe you have me confused with Thomas. Such riffraff, those Steeles.''

''Thomas isn't riffraff,'' she objected. ''He's democratic.''

Worth lifted a quizzical brow. ''If you tell me he was your husband's best friend, I'll go back and apologize.''

Elizabeth thought about how to answer. ''I believe Professor Burns is respected in his field,'' she said carefully. ''Lawrence admired his scholarship.''

''You didn't?''

''Lawrence was brilliant, and I always thought Professor Burns—Gus,'' she choked back a giggle, ''made Lawrence his protégé because he knew Lawrence would go places.''

''And Burns wanted to share the limelight.''

''Yes.'' She added guiltily, ''I have no proof of that.''

''You mean a man can be an obnoxious jerk and still be good at his work?''

''It's possible.''

''I assume when your husband was living, Burns kept his eyes to himself.''

''Of course,'' she lied, and hoped the flush on her face didn't betray her. Lawrence had brushed off Elizabeth's complaints, saying it meant nothing, that Burns looked at all women that way. One of their very few arguments had ensued when Elizabeth said she wished one of the female professors or students would hit Burns with sexual harassment charges.

''I can go back and slug him if you want, but Cheyenne would probably throw a fit if he dripped blood on one of her rugs.''

"You don't need to hit him. I'm sure you sufficiently humiliated him."

"Do I owe you an apology?"

"No."

"Then why the unhappy look on your face? Never mind," he said hastily. "That was thoughtless of me. Seeing someone from the university must be painful. I'm sorry. He rubbed me the wrong way, but my behavior was selfish and inexcusable. You and Professor Burns could have talked over old times, shared some memories of your late husband. I should have left you with him."

"That would have been inexcusable," Elizabeth said firmly. "The man is a highly educated, pompous jerk. I know you were annoyed on Cheyenne's account, and I thoroughly appreciated your sticking pins in him." An unladylike snicker slipped out. "Gus. That must have hurt him the most." Rising on her toes, she gave Worth a quick kiss on his cheek. "Thank you. I'm sure it says something awful about my character, but I enjoyed that."

"You're welcome." His hand rested warmly on her hip. "I have to admit he shows good taste in his ogling."

Blue eyes were supposed to be cold. Not warm and sexy with teasing lights. Elizabeth suddenly had trouble breathing. "He'll ogle anything with two X-chromosomes."

"There are chromosomes and there are chromosomes." Moving his hand to her waist, Worth guided her to the table of food.

Elizabeth stared at a mountain of shrimp with unseeing eyes. Worth's last statement made perfect sense to her. Put X and Y chromosomes together and you had Augustine Burns.

Or Worth Lassiter.

A rugged, good-looking, arrogant, heart-stopping cowboy who'd make a sexy lover and a good father. And no doubt a difficult husband.

Elizabeth had had one husband. She didn't want another.

Lawrence had manipulated her, lied to her and betrayed her.

Maybe that had something to do with the Y-chromosome. She had no desire to explore the subject.

She did, however, want to know what Worth was up to.

Piling food on her plate, he refused to discuss what he'd meant when he'd suggested they come to an arrangement.

Whatever he'd meant, Elizabeth felt sure his proposed arrangement was designed to benefit Worth Lassiter and not Elizabeth Randall.

"Quit stalling," Elizabeth said impatiently the next day, "and tell me about this so-called arrangement, which I know I'm not going to like." Worth probably thought waiting to hear what he had in mind would soften her opposition. He was wrong. "There's no danger of being overheard here. It's just you and me and Jamie in the backseat, and he's not going to tell anyone anything."

Worth looked in the rearview mirror of the extended cab pickup. "Mum's the word, right, Jimbo?"

"Jamie," Elizabeth said automatically.

Jamie kicked his feet and chattered back to Worth. Worth had taught her son to use the mirror to see the driver, and Jamie chortled every time Worth caught his eye. Jamie had adjusted to the ebb and flow of Lassiter family life and was loving every part of it.

Especially Worth.

Elizabeth chose to believe Jamie's adoration of Worth meant nothing more than a little boy needing a man in his life. A teenaged boy lived next door to her in Nebraska. He seemed nice. Perhaps she could hire him to spend time with Jamie after they returned home. Any adult male would suffice.

There was nothing special about Worth Lassiter.

She turned to look at him. His large hat shadowed his forehead, but the sun silhouetted his unyielding jaw, his strong, rugged face. Occasionally, she caught glimpses of him in his sisters' faces and them in his. Funny how the same parts could look so feminine on them and so masculine on him. Like his mouth. All four of them had the same generous mouth. A mouth made for laughing.

And kissing.

Elizabeth wished she could forget the feel of his mouth. Firm, yet tender. But not for her.

"Why the sigh?"

"No sigh." Hopefully he wouldn't notice the heat she felt on her face. "I didn't sigh. If I did, it was because I was wondering if you were ever going to satisfy my curiosity."

The air in the car immediately vibrated with hidden meaning, and Elizabeth knew without a doubt Worth had chosen to interpret her words in a sexually provocative way.

"I assume you mean about us coming to an arrangement?"

"Of course I mean that," she snapped. "Do you think about anything but sex?"

He looked at her from beneath elevated eyebrows before saying seriously, "I think it has something to do with ions or electrons or something like that."

"What are you talking about?"

"Take lightning. Electricity flashing from one place to another. It's probably your red hair. The question is, is red hair a generator or a conductor?"

"I think," she said tightly, "you're dodging the issue."

"You're the one who brought up sex. I was looking for an explanation for all this zinging going on between us."

"I did not bring up sex." She refused to discuss nonexistent zinging. She didn't zing. "All I said was I wanted you to satisfy..." The mirthful quirk at the corner of his mouth stopped her. "Never mind. Just tell me what you were talking about last night."

"Okay." He slid a gloved finger along the rim of the steering wheel.

The movement shrieked of sexual overtones. Her skin tingled as if he was running his finger over her. The way it had tingled when he'd said Professor Burns showed good taste in ogling. Not because of what he'd said, but because of the male appreciation in his eyes at the time. Elizabeth clamped her teeth. She would not allow tingling.

"Why won't you tell Russ you're afraid of horses?" Worth asked.

All tingling immediately ceased. "Your big arrangement is more blackmail? None of your business. And I'm not afraid of horses."

He wore sunglasses, but the skin around his eyes wrinkled as if he were squinting in concentrated thought. "Okay," he said eventually. "I'll go first. Then you can tell me."

"There's nothing to tell."

"Russ said your stepfather is in the military so you've lived all over the world." At her nod, he continued. "And that fancy hotel chain you work for has moved you several times."

He didn't say anything for a long time, as if marshaling his thoughts. Elizabeth couldn't even begin to guess where this conversation was headed.

"Cheyenne and Allie attended colleges back east," he said. "Greeley could have, but she chose to go to Colorado State. I went to Grand Junction, a couple hours west of here, so I could come home weekends, sometimes even overnight, depending on my class schedule. Grandpa Yancy was gone then, and boys were starting to notice Cheyenne. Mom told all of us about the birds and the bees, but I needed to be here so the guys coming around would know they couldn't pull anything. I know what teenaged boys are like, and Mom is too easygoing and trusting. My sisters, especially Cheyenne, threw a fit about my 'big brother act', as they called it, but someone had to protect them."

Elizabeth visualized Worth pacing the porch, waiting for his sisters to return home safely. She had no trouble imagining him as protective. And inflexible. "I'll bet you were a real pain."

He grinned. "At least three people thought so."

"I'm sure they still do." That was a lie. His sisters complained, but it was clear they exaggerated their complaints and obviously adored him. Which they were demonstrating by their loving, if misguided, efforts to find him a wife.

Elizabeth had sided with them, not because she thought Worth's single state was any of their business, but because she didn't like being used.

"We've had our moments, but they survived." Satisfaction filled his voice, making him sound like a proud papa.

"You may not survive if you don't explain what you meant last night about a mutual arrangement."

"Have you ever been to China?" he asked in a total change of subject. "Seen the Great Wall?"

"No." Elizabeth inwardly sighed. She had a feeling Worth was never going to tell her his stupid plan. He must have had second thoughts. "My stepfather was never stationed in the Far East."

"Have you ever thought about walking on it? Imagined what it would be like building it?" Obviously the question was rhetorical because he continued, "I've never been to Asia. Never been to Europe. Never walked on a California beach. I want to hike the Appalachian Trail. Stand in the middle of Times Square in New York City. See the Great Barrier Reef. Alaskan glaciers. There's always been this sort of hole in my life. A sense of something missing. A restlessness. So much I've never done, so many places I've never been. Sights I've never seen."

He glanced fleetingly at her, then looked straight ahead. "Now Mom and my sisters have someone to take care of them. As for the ranch, after fifteen years of managing that big spread down in Texas, Russ can handle any ranch business while I'm gone. There's no reason I can't take off now and again. Have adventures. Take chances. Live life."

A picture began to take shape for Elizabeth. One of unselfish devotion to his family. "You want to do things you couldn't do before, because you were helping raise your sisters."

"I don't regret for one second what I did for Mom and my sisters," he said quickly, "but now they're married. I'm not hobbled by family responsibilities."

The last piece of the picture snapped into place. "And the last thing you want is to get married."

"The very last. Someday, sure, but not now. Now I'm looking forward to doing the things I've never been able to do."

"Which is why you were hiding behind an fake relationship with me last night."

He flashed her an enigmatic glance. "Whatever."

"Tell your sisters the truth. That you don't want to get married because you want to do other things first."

His mouth thinned in disgust. "I thought you were smarter than that. They'd think I resented them, think I made sacrifices for them. I didn't, but no matter how I explain it, it sounds as if I think I did. You don't understand what I mean and neither would they. I won't have them feeling guilty. I'm not a martyr and I didn't make sacrifices. I did what I had to do, and I don't regret any of it. If I had to, I'd do it again. But I don't have to, and I don't intend to tie myself down with a wife. Not now. Now I intend to expand my horizons. So there it is." He looked expectantly at her. "Okay, it's your turn to divulge your deep, dark secret."

Elizabeth almost panicked. He couldn't know. Russ didn't know. No one knew. "I don't have a secret," she said quickly, "Whoever told you I did, lied. I'm not telling you anything. You made all that stuff up so I'd tell you, but I'm not going to tell you." She took a deep breath to calm herself. "There's nothing to tell."

Worth spliced the last strand of broken wire and threw the fence stretcher into the back of the pickup. Repairing fence wasn't his favorite chore and he usually left it to his men, but today he didn't mind the work. It occupied his hands and left his mind free to puzzle over Elizabeth's strange reaction to his question. He'd wanted to know why she didn't tell Russ about her fear of horses. The way she'd practically bounced off the inside of the pickup made him wonder what she thought he'd been asking.

Her reaction forcibly reminded him of when his sister Allie

was ten and she stole a wretched little male dog after seeing his abusive owner beat him bloody. She'd hidden the half-dead animal in the barn, caring for him on the sly. Guilt over the theft had preyed on her until the day Worth asked her something about cleaning out a stall and she'd gone ballistic, yelling about people who ignored evil when they had big barns. Until then, Worth had had no idea about their illicit guest.

He wondered what guilty secret plagued Elizabeth.

They'd hauled the playpen in the truck with them, and it now sat in the shade of a large pine while Jamie slept, his bottom sticking up in the air. Elizabeth sat cross-legged on a large blanket near her son, a book in her lap. Either she was a very slow reader or her mind was elsewhere.

Something troubled Elizabeth. Finding out what ought to be her father's job, but not only was Russ tied up with wedding plans and the loose ends from the Texas ranch, he wasn't exactly skilled at communicating with his daughter.

Stifling a sigh, Worth ambled over to the blanket and stretched out full length. "Jimbo has a good idea," he said quietly so he wouldn't awaken the baby. He tipped his hat down over his face.

Elizabeth didn't respond. No surprise. She hadn't said much of anything to him since denying she had any secrets. It must be a barn-burner of a secret.

"Just so you know, Red, blackmail won't work on me." He sensed her startled reaction.

"What's that supposed to mean?"

"I trusted you with something I've never told anyone else. If you think you can use my secret against me, you can't."

A red-winged blackbird called from some reeds down the road. He heard Elizabeth close her book.

"Why can't I?" she asked slowly.

"I'll deny it."

"Why did you tell me?"

"Horse-trading. I tell you something; you tell me something. I tell you why I don't want to get married. You tell me why you won't tell Russ about your fear of horses."

The pause was longer this time.

"That's what you wanted me to tell you?"

He lifted his hat and give her a quizzical look. "What else?"

"Nothing else," she said quickly.

Her hasty denial confirmed his suspicions. Whatever Elizabeth was hiding, it had nothing to do with telling Russ about her fear of horses. He watched a host of emotions parade across her face. Some like doubt and mistrust and fear he recognized. Others were less easily identified. "You can trust me, Red," he said. "Look at it this way. Confiding my secret to you was the same as handing you a weapon you could use against me."

"I thought you said you'd deny telling me anything."

"I would, but that wouldn't keep my sisters from stewing about it. I gave you the power to hurt my whole family."

"Why?"

"To prove I trust you." He replaced his hat over his face.

"That's dirty pool," she said in a low, annoyed voice.

He grinned under his hat. The ploy always worked with his sisters. They grudgingly came clean when he told them how much he trusted them.

"What makes you think you can trust me?"

"Jimbo. The way you are with him. He trusts you."

"His name is Jamie and he's just a baby. His trusting someone is hardly a recommendation. After all, he trusts you."

"So he does." Worth could almost hear the thoughts scurrying around in her head. In a nearby field, magpies squabbled. His eyes sank closed, then Elizabeth took a deep breath, and he snapped to attention.

"When my parents divorced, Russ told me he and my mother were getting a divorce because they were totally different. He said he was a cowboy and Mother was a city person. I said I was going to live in a city, and he said where I lived didn't matter, but I knew even then he and I were different." She fell silent.

Worth knew there had to be more. He waited.

"Russ said all those differences wouldn't matter." She hesitated. "He said we'd always have our love of horses to bind us together."

Hiding her fear of horses from Russ made sense now. In a weird sort of way. No doubt Russ's words had been well-meant, his intent to reassure his little girl. Unfortunately they'd had the opposite effect. Behind Elizabeth's reluctant explanation, Worth sensed the little girl who worried her daddy wouldn't love her when he found out she didn't like horses. Sometimes the most irrational fears had the longest roots. Only Russ could reassure his daughter he'd love her no matter what, a reassurance Russ wouldn't give because he didn't know it was needed.

"You think it's a stupid hang-up," Elizabeth burst out when Worth didn't immediately respond. "That I think my father can't love me if he knows I'm afraid of horses, and if he can't, then I shouldn't care what he thinks. Maybe that was true when I was little, but it's more complicated than that now."

"Life usually is," Worth said neutrally.

"Maybe he hasn't been the best father, but maybe I haven't been the best daughter either. You don't want your family feeling guilty. Well, I don't want Russ feeling guilty either. I know he worries he's been a bad father. I know it bothers him that I'm closer to my stepfather than I am to him. Some things just are. I didn't plan it. It's easier talking to my stepfather. Russ isn't the easiest person to talk to unless you're talking cows or horses or you are another cowboy. And before you blame me, I've tried to be the daughter he wants."

Worth lifted his hat. "I'm not passing judgment on you. This isn't about passing judgments It's about leverage."

She gave him a guarded look. "Leverage?"

Good. He'd turned her thoughts. Worth assumed an innocent air and grinned engagingly. Her eyes narrowed suspiciously. Maybe she wasn't as naive as he thought. "You're spending too much time with my sisters."

"Because I don't trust you?"

What was it about her lips that fascinated him? He dragged his thoughts back to the business at hand. "I know you're afraid of horses and you don't want Russ to know.'' He held up a hand when she would have interrupted. ''You know I'm looking forward with great anticipation to shedding my family responsibilities and you know I don't want my family knowing how I feel. With me so far?''

''Maybe.''

The noncommittal answer brought another smile to his face. His sisters must have really laid it on.

''I suppose we're back to the blackmail.'' She'd misinterpreted the smile.

''You can call it mutual blackmail if you want. I prefer to think of it as working to each other's benefit.''

''I'm sure you do.''

Jamie made a sound in his sleep, catching his mother's attention. She turned to him, adjusting the light blanket over him, her face warm and gentle with love.

Her softened lips parted. Worth quit resisting temptation. Sitting up in one fluid movement, he leaned toward her and corralled her face. She gave him a startled look before quickly closing her eyes as he bent his head and planted a firm kiss on her surprised mouth. Backing off, Worth congratulated himself on his superhuman self-control.

''What was that for?'' she asked breathlessly.

''You mean it doesn't happen all the time? When you're walking down the street, perfect strangers don't walk up to you and kiss that mouth?'' He traced her bottom lip with his thumb. ''It's such a kissable mouth.'' Her cheeks lit up like the breast of the robin sitting on the nearest fence post. Worth wondered if the rest of her lit up when a man kissed her all over.

She pushed aside his hand. ''You're changing the subject again.''

Worth resumed his reclining position on the blanket, his hat over his face. ''You gave me the idea last night. We team up. I thwart Russ's efforts to get you on a horse, and you thwart my sisters' efforts to hobble me with some woman.''

''Exactly how am I supposed to do that?''

"Simple. If I'm involved with you, I can't be involved with someone else."

The robin broadcast his cheery song to the skies. In the distance a cow mooed. Worth smelled the earth and the grass and the pine trees. And he waited.

"You're not involved with me," Elizabeth finally said.

"All that counts is whether people think I am."

"Your sisters won't believe you are for a minute."

"Nope, they won't. The other women will. Cheyenne will assume I'm being deliberately obstructive."

"Which you are."

"Sure I am. When she sees me using you to block her plans, she'll hopefully realize I'm delivering a message to her to stay out of my life. A message she'd never get if all I do is ignore the women she keeps parading before me."

"It would be a lot simpler to tell her you aren't interested in getting married now. You don't have to tell her why."

Worth snorted in disgust from under his hat. "That simple-minded remark shows how little you know about my sister. Cheyenne is a grade-A meddler, who always knows what's best for everyone else. Unfortunately, she's been right a couple of times, and it's gone to her head," he added grimly.

"In other words, Cheyenne has a record of successfully meddling," Elizabeth gave a choked laugh, "and you're scared."

"Darned right I am. Cheyenne turning her attention to me is a man's worst nightmare. She's underhanded and she's got two sisters for backup. My only option is to outmaneuver her. Our arrangement would put her off her stride. I'm not talking a long-term relationship here. Just long enough to make my point that I want her to mind her own business. Nothing will stop her for long, but after the wedding I can use ranch business as an excuse to avoid her, and when Russ and Mom come back from their honeymoon, I'll start my travels. So, what do you say?"

"Your sisters have already warned me you're only using me to hide behind. I'd look like an idiot."

He lifted his hat. "No, you won't." He paused for effect. "You tell them I'm blackmailing you into playing along."

"You have tried to blackmail me."

"That's why it's the perfect answer. You don't have to lie."

"They'd want to know why you're blackmailing me."

"No, they won't. They're irritating, but they're not stupid. The whole point of blackmail is you have a secret you don't want told. If you could tell, you couldn't be blackmailed. I've known my sisters all their lives. I know how they think. Not only will they not ask what your secret is, they'll rally around you. I'm the one who should be worried, not you."

She didn't look convinced. "So why aren't you?"

"Because it's a foolproof plan."

"What about Russ and your mom?"

"If they notice anything besides each other, Mom will assume I'm being a good host and Russ will think you're interested in the ranch, which would seem logical to him."

"Your sisters will tell your mother what's going on."

Worth shook his head. "Years ago the four of us agreed there was no need to worry Mom over insignificant details."

"Insignificant details," she echoed in a hollow voice.

Worth could see Elizabeth needed some time to get used to his plan.

CHAPTER FIVE

THE next day Elizabeth eyed Worth critically as he sat behind the pickup's steering wheel. A man had no right looking that good when all he was doing was going out to check on a few animals.

Yesterday Worth had almost persuaded her. Not by his logic. By raising his hat and unleashing his killer smile. Elizabeth hated how much his smile affected her stomach. He had no right to smile at her like that. As if he meant it. When she knew he was only trying to manipulate her.

With that smile he could sell ice to polar bears.

She refused to think how close he'd come to selling her on his ridiculous scheme. Not for any of the nonsensical reasons he'd given, but for reasons which had popped up of their own accord in her head.

Silly reasons. Childish reasons. Selfish reasons.

Reasons which tempted and seduced.

A harmless game of pretense.

For the rest of her visit, she could pretend she was someone else. Pretend she was a desirable woman, the kind a man cherished. Pretend a man saw her as a woman he wanted to know, a woman he loved for herself, not because she was an extension of someone else.

She wouldn't be a woman he feared would sabotage her father's upcoming marriage for vengeful reasons. She could forget she was a freckled redhead.

Forget she was a lonely, abandoned widow.

What could be the harm in that kind of pretending?

It would be for only a few days. A game.

Worth wouldn't need to know the game she played. It was a game one could play.

Lawrence had taught her that.

"Do you always have this much trouble making up your mind?"

"I already told you no," Elizabeth said.

"You didn't mean it."

"Were you born arrogant or do you have to work at it?"

"It's impossible to be arrogant when you have three sisters ready and willing to point out your every flaw."

"You've accomplished the impossible."

"If I can get you to agree with me about how we can act to our mutual benefit, I'll believe that," he said.

"Not interested." Common sense had finally reasserted itself, and Elizabeth ruthlessly banished from her mind the idea of playing games of any kind with Worth. Behind the arrogance, the good looks, the older-brother attitude, the sexy smiles, the kisses, was a man who'd managed the family ranch since before he was twenty. Elizabeth knew from Russ the kind of toughness needed to run an operation of this size. She wasn't tough enough to play games with a man like Worth Lassiter.

He frowned at the road ahead. Before she could ask what the problem was, Worth muttered under his breath and brought the pickup to a halt. "Stay in the truck," he said briefly, climbing out and quietly closing the door.

Looking past him, Elizabeth saw a bay mare and a small foal by the pasture fence. The mare pawed at the ground and whinnied in Worth's direction, before nickering urgently at the foal. Elizabeth saw what Worth had already seen. The foal had one leg caught in the fence. Worth's soothing voice came through the open window. The foal twitched a couple of times, making distressed sounds that aroused Elizabeth's pity. Tossing her head, the mare nickered softly back.

Worth went to the mare first, touching her and talking quietly. Even from the pickup Elizabeth could sense the horse's trust in Worth. The mare's forehead seemed wrinkled in anxiety, but she followed calmly as Worth moved to her foal's side. He rubbed the tiny horse's neck, but made no move toward the snared leg. The foal appeared exhausted, its eyes half closed as it leaned against Worth.

Giving the baby one last pat, Worth returned to the pickup. "I need some help here, Red. Russ is tied up on the phone with those idiots down in Texas who thought any lamebrain could run a ranch, and Mom's playing kissy-face with Jimbo."

Mary had insisted, but Elizabeth felt guilty about allowing herself to be persuaded. "His name is Jamie, and I should have brought him or stayed at the ranch, instead of expecting your mom to baby-sit."

"Why do you think she insisted you come with me? She wanted Jimbo to herself." He made a dismissive gesture. "Forget that now. I might be able to reach one of the men on the cell phone, but nobody's close. The foal's leg doesn't look too bad, but if he's startled, he's likely to break a bone or rip a bunch of tendons. I'll halter Susie, but there's no safe place to tie the mare."

Elizabeth shook her head. She knew what he was going to ask and there was no way she could do it.

"I need you to hold the mare so she stays out of the way and doesn't make things worse."

"I can't."

"Susie's as gentle as they come, and I don't think you'll have any problem with her."

"You don't think?" She couldn't hide the panic in her voice.

"She's a horse," he said patiently. "I don't know what happened here, and I don't know what she's thinking, what kind of fears she has. Susie's intelligent, and I think she'll understand I'm trying to help the little guy, and she'll trust me to do it. I'll put on the halter, lead her a little way off, where she can watch what's going on, but she can't accidentally bump or kick the foal."

"Kick the foal! What about me?"

He gave her a long, steady look. "I wouldn't ask you to help if I thought I'd be putting you in danger, but I can't make any guarantees."

Elizabeth scuttled into the far corner of the passenger seat. "I can't help you."

"You can."

"I'm not going near those horses."

"I have to get some things out of the back. Join us when you're ready." Worth turned and walked behind the pickup. Metallic sounds came from the pickup's bed.

The mare whinnied again. The foal answered fretfully. Like Jamie when he fell and wanted his mama to make his hurt go away. Elizabeth pleated the front of her trousers with her fingers. They weren't her horses. If the mare was so gentle, she wouldn't bother Worth.

If he really needed her assistance, he would have lied, told her she'd be perfectly all right. Told her Susie would never in a million years bite her or kick her. He would have argued more. Threatened Elizabeth. Dragged her to the pasture.

Not just assumed she'd do as he asked. Assumed she could do it. Elizabeth stared straight ahead, refusing to look toward the pasture.

She couldn't do it.

Metal clanked and Worth's measured footsteps walked away.

Susie was a stupid name for a horse.

The foal's cries of distress sounded almost like a baby crying.

The door handle was icy cold against her palm. Elizabeth left the truck door unlatched so she didn't startle the horses and forced herself to walk slowly toward the pasture.

Worth heard her dragging footsteps approaching through the pasture grass, but he didn't turn. Experience had taught him that trying to talk a person out of a deep-seated fear only infuriated the person. And lent weight to the fear.

Funny how a person would argue forever about doing something, but if you just assumed they'd do it, they often would.

Elizabeth didn't give herself enough credit.

Worth fastened the halter on the mare and thought about

Elizabeth the first time he'd seen her at the Denver airport. The weariness. The shadowed eyes. The rail-thin body. The straight, brittle spine. The way she carried the weight of her world on her shoulders.

The way she smiled for her son. Was strong for Jamie.

Elizabeth's inner core of strength was obvious to everyone but her. Worth could tell her it was there, but she'd never believe him. He had to show her.

He prayed he was right.

"I'll walk Susie over here where she can watch the foal," Worth said, still refusing to turn around. If he saw terror on her face, he'd send her back to the truck. Further reinforcing her fear. "Stand here, and hold on to Susie here." He placed Elizabeth's hand. "Don't move between her and the foal and don't watch what I'm doing. Watch her. Let me know if she starts showing increased signs of distress." He tried to speak in a calm, matter-of-fact voice.

He could almost feel the rapid, panicky beat of her heart. A word of kindness and Elizabeth would collapse. Ignoring the upheaval in his stomach, Worth reminded himself Susie was about as well-behaved as a horse could be. "And watch your feet so Susie doesn't accidentally step on them." He gave Elizabeth a quick squeeze on her shoulder and left, to take care of the colt as quickly as possible.

The mare was huge. After one dubious look at Elizabeth, the mother horse concentrated all her attention on Worth and her foal. Her ears pointed straight ahead. It seemed to Elizabeth concern filled the large brown eyes. On impulse, she said gently, "Your baby will be okay. Worth will take care of him." The mare turned her gaze back to Elizabeth.

She forced herself not to back up, and continued in a soft voice. "I have a baby boy, too. His name is Jamie. It's incredible the trouble little boys can get into, isn't it? Jamie keeps trying to walk before he can figure out the balance thing and he falls down on his bottom all the time. But little boys are tough. They always bounce back. Your baby will be just fine.'' As she babbled on, the mare became less a frightening monster and more another worried mother.

"Here we go, Susie. One little guy who's starving." Worth guided the foal to his mother's side. "You can let go now," he said as the foal butted the mare, then eagerly suckled.

"No, I can't. My fingers won't move."

Worth gently pried open her hand and unsnapped the rope from the mare's halter. "I won't say a word if you want to scramble over the fence."

She leaned against him, her legs as shaky as the exhausted foal's. "Why?"

"Now the crisis is over, the rest of the gang is coming over to say hello."

Elizabeth's eyes widened at the sight of a dozen or so mares ambling toward them. Foals, kicking up their heels, scampered ahead of their moms. Elizabeth scaled the fence in record time.

Worth moved to meet the horses, greeting the mares first, rubbing and patting them, before he touched the foals.

Elizabeth dropped to the pickup's running board on the driver's side, her legs feeling like overcooked noodles. Stretching them in front of her, she sat like a lump and watched Worth as he made his way around the crowd of babies, scratching necks, rubbing his hand over their heads and faces, picking up their feet. The mares looked on indulgently. If one nickered, Worth pushed her baby toward her. After a last round of attention to the mares, Worth headed back toward the pickup.

The injured foal sported a front leg wrapped in bright pink. "Will he be okay?" Elizabeth asked.

"He was lucky. Only a tiny scrape," Worth said from behind the truck. "I put some antiseptic on it, and we'll keep an eye on him. Thanks for helping."

She waited for him to praise her courage.

He came around the truck. "Here." He poured water on her hands from the thermos, then handed her a clean hanky. "Hold out your hand. Waterless antibiotic soap."

She dutifully accepted the liquid gel and rubbed. The sharp smell assaulted her nose as the soap evaporated, chilling her skin. In the face of Worth's silence, Elizabeth's euphoria over facing her fear, if only for a short duration, evaporated.

Anger replaced it. The least he could do was acknowledge her tiny bit of courage. "Don't bother to pat me on the back or anything," she snapped. "Never mind I was shaking like a leaf out there. Never mind I absolutely did not want to go anywhere near your stupid horses. Never mind that your dumb horse might have bitten off my arm, or—"

"Susie doesn't bite," Worth interjected mildly.

"—or trampled my feet or kicked my head off. Never mind any of that. The great Worth Lassiter expects instant compliance with his wishes."

"I wouldn't exactly call it instant," he drawled in a teasing voice.

Elizabeth was in no mood to be teased. She jumped to her feet to walk away. After one step, her toe caught in a deep rut in the road.

Worth caught her around her waist before she fell. "Could you give me a clue here what you're so mad about?" His arm stayed around her waist as he turned her to face him.

Holding her body rigidly erect, Elizabeth clutched his arms, for balance. And to keep distance between them. "You know very well I'm afraid of horses."

"You bragging?"

How did a man get to be so arrogant and insensitive? "I'm not bragging. I'm just saying. I'm afraid of horses, but I helped you."

"And I thanked you."

"You're so dumb you have no idea what I'm talking about."

"Sure I do." He tipped up her chin. "You think you did something totally out of character and I should be surprised."

If she stared much harder at his top shirt button she'd go cross-eyed. "I did do something out of character. I'm afraid of horses."

"What is that, your mantra or something?" He wrapped his

hands around her face. "I wasn't the least bit surprised by what you did. I knew you'd help."

"I suppose you thought I'd help because you told me to," she said angrily. Anger would drive away the feel of work-toughened hands. Keep her from rubbing her cheek against his warm palm. "I have news for you. I didn't do it for you. I wouldn't cross the street for you."

"You did it because it had to be done. And because you're a mother and you couldn't sit by and watch a baby suffer."

His words took some of the heat from her anger. "You took my compliance for granted," she said lamely.

"No, I took your strength and courage for granted." He trailed his thumb across her cheekbone.

Surprised, her gaze shot up to his face. To see eyes warm with approval. "Oh." Pinching his shirt sleeve between her thumb and forefinger, she rubbed the faded blue chambray fabric. And wondered if every shade of blue she saw the rest of her life would remind her of his eyes.

"When I first saw you in Denver at the airport, I thought you looked as if life had knocked all the stuffing out of you, leaving nothing but skin and bones. It didn't take me long to learn how stubborn you were, but I assumed the first breath of wind that came along would knock you over. I was wrong. You might look puny—"

His unflattering assessment stung. "I am not puny."

He ignored her protest. "Inside where it counts, you're tough as boot leather. Mom raised four kids pretty much on her own, and I know the love and strength that took. I've watched you with Jimbo. You have that same reservoir of strength and courage. You'll be just fine."

Perversely, his vote of confidence pleased her no more than his initial negative assumption. "Don't patronize me. I don't need you to pat me on the back and tell me I'll be fine. If I decide I'll be fine, I'll be fine."

He smiled. "I don't want to fight with you."

Elizabeth wondered how long his killer smile would haunt

her dreams. "You don't want to fight because you're afraid you'll lose."

His smile slipped. "Yeah, I'd lose." The wry expression on his face faded away as he eyed her with a lazy sensuality.

Her fingers tightened on his arms. Why hadn't she let go? Walked away.

Her hat was in the truck and the sun warmed the back of her head. With her every breath came his scent, a mixture of soap, horse and male. A soft breeze danced through the roadside weeds and overhead leaves, lifting a few strands of her hair. Mothers and foals called softly to each other in the pasture. A hummingbird whistled past.

Worth's intense gaze fixed on her face. As if he was memorizing her features. Or waiting. Was she supposed to kiss him first? Send him a written invitation? Throw him to the ground and straddle his body? She dug her fingers into his hard muscles and parted her lips to demand he kiss her.

The only sound she uttered was a small moan of mingled anticipation and satisfaction as he came down on her mouth, hot and heavy and demanding. His large metal belt buckle pressed against her middle, and she felt the muscled strength of his arms and the hardness of his thighs.

Elizabeth leaned into the kiss, exulting in the feelings which swept through her. She felt alive. Greedily, she wanted it all. The taste of his mouth, his tongue. She went on her tiptoes, pressing her hands to the back of his neck. A rainbow of sensations flooded her. He felt good, smelled good, tasted good.

Worth lifted his head. "A truck's coming," he said, his voice thick.

Hearing the hum of tires, she stepped back, inordinately pleased with the realization he'd been reluctant to break off the kiss. Had the sky been that blue earlier? So many birds singing?

Sweet clover from the other side of the road perfumed the air, its blossoms gloriously yellow. The pickup slowed in passing, the driver lifting his hand in a brief salute. The dust settled on Worth's shirt. Elizabeth refrained from brushing it off and gave him a slightly embarrassed glance. She'd never before kissed a man in the middle of a public road.

He gazed steadily back. "I won't deny you intrigue me, Red." A slight frown creased his brow. "Under other circumstances I'd be tempted to pursue some kind of relationship with you, but now's not the right time. I'm sorry."

For a moment Elizabeth could only stare at him, stunned at his interpretation of their kiss. Leave it to a man to ruin everything. "Right time for what? Kissing out in the middle of nowhere?"

A crooked smile of regret passed fleetingly over his mouth. "You know what I mean. I'm not ready to settle down, to make a long-term commitment, and you're not a woman who'd accept anything less."

Now he'd really gone too far. "You're warning me away from you? Are you so conceited you actually think I've fallen in love with you?"

"Don't get excited." Worth stuck his hands in the air and backed away. "I'm just making sure we're both clear on where we stand."

His words failed to mollify her. "What makes you think you're so wonderful that when a woman kisses you," Elizabeth jabbed him in the chest with her finger, "you automatically assume she's after your body or a wedding ring? Let me tell you something, Worth Lassiter—"

She jabbed him again. "I've been married once. I'm not looking to repeat the experience. Maybe I'm the one who ought to be worried. That kiss was all your idea, and don't you dare say different. You wanted to kiss me as much as... Never mind, the point is, you wanted to kiss me."

He grabbed her finger and held it still. "As much as what? As much as you wanted to hold Susie? As much as Jimbo wants his breakfast in the morning? Or as much as you wanted to kiss me?"

Heat flooded her face. "All right," she said, daring him to make something of it, "as much as I wanted to kiss you. All of a sudden I felt really good. I haven't felt really good in a long time, and I needed an outlet to express how good I felt. Kissing seemed a good idea. I don't make a practice of kissing blockheads, but it was you or a horse, and even you rate over horses.'' Showing him her back, she stomped around the pickup and climbed into the passenger seat. At the last second, she remembered the horses and refrained from slamming the door.

Dust trailed behind the pickup as they traveled down the gravel road. Inside the truck's cab, a rigid, uncomfortable silence prevailed.

Folding her hands in her lap, Elizabeth studied the tracery of blue veins beneath her pale skin. And in her mind saw Worth's tanned hands reaching for her naked body.

Her instincts told her he'd be a wonderful, satisfying lover. But not her lover.

Besides, she had lousy instincts.

''Before Susie's foal distracted us, we were discussing the mutual benefits of our arrangement.''

''I am not pretending to be your girlfriend because you're afraid of your sisters. And after I helped you today you can't claim I'm afraid of horses. No one would believe you.''

''That's your final say?''

''Positively final, and I don't want to discuss it again.''

After a few minutes Worth started whistling a popular country tune. Elizabeth basked in her triumph for about six seconds. Then she remembered what his sisters said. Worth always got his way.

''I feel so badly about how this trip has gone for you,'' Mary said, driving them back to the ranch after a ladies-only luncheon.

Elizabeth gave the older woman an apprehensive look. What had Worth said to his mother? ''I'm not sure what you mean.''

''This mess with those people in Texas. Just because the ranch has been in their family for years, those idiot grandsons decided they could operate the spread themselves. I swear they thought ranching was nine-to-five with weekends off. You came to spend some time with your father, and he's being forced to spend all his time on the phone holding their hands.''

''That's okay. I understand,'' Elizabeth said. She could hardly tell Mary every visit with Russ went pretty much the same way, Russ paying more attention to work than to his daughter. ''I'm happy to have the opportunity to get acquainted with you and your family.'' She hesitated. ''I know Russ'll be in good hands with you.''

Mary raised a quizzical brow, demonstrating exactly where her son had learned the habit. ''Is that a subtle way of saying I'm a managing woman?''

''I think Russ needs a little managing,'' Elizabeth said impulsively. ''Mom expected him to know what she wanted, what she thought. You tell him straight out. I expect he finds that helpful.''

''I expect he does,'' Mary agreed with mock solemnity.

Elizabeth couldn't help but laugh. She'd seen from the beginning how good Mary was for Russ. No matter what Worth thought, Elizabeth was happy for them both.

''I'm afraid,'' Mary said, turning serious again, ''we're rather a straight-talking family, which can take a little getting used to. I hope we haven't put you off us.''

''You've all been very kind. Having Jamie and me here now must be a nuisance.''

''I'd hoped we'd have more time together. I've married off three daughters; you'd think I'd have the drill down by now. I thought we'd have a simple little wedding, just family, but my family goes way back in the area, and we know a lot of people around the state, and things ballooned.'' She sighed. ''You've been so good about me sending you off with Worth, which is the best I've been able to do to entertain you. So many details. Thank goodness for Jamie. He keeps me sane.''

''I hope Worth can say the same by the time the wedding's over,'' Elizabeth said guiltily. ''He's been stuck with Jamie a lot this week.'' She could have left Jamie with Cheyenne's nanny, but Worth had insisted Jamie stay with him.

''Worth adores children. Even when he was a child himself.

Not many ten-year-old boys willingly watch over their younger sisters. Worth would read to the girls, oversee their teeth brushing, whatever was needed. He's been my Rock of Gibraltar.''

When they reached the ranch house, Russ waved from Worth's office, the phone glued to his ear. There was no sign of Jamie or the Rock of Gibraltar. Elizabeth went in search while Mary joined Russ.

Male laughter led her through the kitchen to the glassed-in back porch. She stood inside the back door, looking out at a small area of green grass surrounded by fruit trees. In the center of the lawn, Worth, his bent knees practically touching his chest, sat with Jamie in a child's plastic wading pool.

As Elizabeth watched silently, Jamie slapped at the water and looked up for Worth's approval. Worth responded with a small wave directed toward Jamie's stomach. Her son laughed gleefully, patting his stomach with his hands. Then he leaned forward, dropping to his hands and knees and scurried over to Worth, where he scaled him like a tree. Worth hugged the little boy, his deep laughter mingling with the child's giggles.

The scene blurred and Elizabeth turned away, biting her lower lip. This was how it was supposed to be. The nine months she'd carried her precious cargo, this was how she'd visualized their future. Her child, cherished by his father.

While a teenager, she'd cried a storm of tears when her stepfather had received transfer orders right after she'd been elected to a high school office for the next year. Her stepfather had been sympathetic, but they had moved before the school year began. The advice he'd given her then echoed in her ear. "Change what you can, Elizabeth. Learn to live with what you can't.''

She dabbed at her eyes, took a deep breath and opened the door.

Worth was encouraging Jamie to stamp his feet in the water.

"I hope he understands what's acceptable in wading pools doesn't cut it in the bathtub," Elizabeth said severely.

Jamie got so excited at the sound of her voice, he would have fallen except for Worth's secure grasp.

"We had a long discussion about that before we got in the pool, and Jimbo assured me he's clear on the difference."

"I'm sure," Elizabeth said dryly, holding out her arms.

"He's soaking wet." Clasping her son to his chest, Worth uncoiled his legs and stood, water streaming down his body.

Jamie's diapers and rubber pants held so much water, they sagged below his bottom. Worth wore wet, boxy bathing trunks, slung low around his hips. There any similarity between the two ended.

Sunlight glistened off Worth's wet skin as he bent over to remove Jamie's diapers. Wide shoulders, narrow waist, trim hips. Strong, powerful legs. Elizabeth wanted to run her fingers over his shoulder blades and back as his muscles flexed. A tanned, beautiful back. The kind a woman could cuddle up to at night. In her imagination, she felt the warmth of his skin.

Worth straightened, laughing as he cradled the naked, wet, squirming baby to his bare chest with large, capable hands.

Elizabeth blinked rapidly in the strong sunlight. Jamie looked so happy. So content. So safe.

"Here you go, Red. One waterlogged Jimbo looking for his mom." Worth handed Jamie to her, her son cocooned in a large, colorful towel. Only his beaming face peeked out.

"Thank you for watching him."

Worth wrapped a towel around his hips and cocked an eyebrow at her. "Don't feel obliged to return the favor."

Elizabeth immediately fired up. "If you thought watching Jamie for me for a couple of hours would convince me to pretend I'm your girlfriend to protect you from your sisters' matchmaking scheme, you thought wrong."

Gently tickling under Jamie's chin, Worth gave her a crooked smile. "I was teasing you. I watched Jimbo because I like him." He walked by her into the house.

Leaving Elizabeth overcome with guilt as Mary Lassiter's words echoed in her head. Worth had been his mother's Rock of Gibraltar. Rocks were always there. Steady, uncomplaining. Supportive.

What kind of person refused to help someone who'd made sure his little sisters brushed their teeth?

"By the way." Worth opened the back screen door and stuck his head out. "The horse you're riding tomorrow is named Rosie."

The look on Elizabeth's face had almost made Worth tell her he was kidding, but he'd bitten back the words. Mollycoddling her was no way to help her fight her fear. If you had a horse who'd developed an irrational fear, you taught the horse to unlearn the fear by gradually approaching the source of the fear until the horse learned for itself there was nothing to be afraid of.

Even allowing for a father's natural tendency to brag about his child, Russ's remarks told Worth that Elizabeth knew how to ride. She'd simply been mounted on horses beyond her abilities, which had resulted in frightening and painful experiences.

All Worth had to do was replace her painful memories with positive experiences. "I'm counting on you, Rosie," he said, laughing when the mare responded with a reassuring nicker. "She knows how to ride. She just needs to gain some confidence."

Leaning on the corral, he scratched under Rosie's chin and throat and thought about the changes in Elizabeth since she'd arrived in Colorado. Not that the visit was turning a coward into a brave woman. He was pretty sure Elizabeth had never been a coward, but life had set her back on her heels, and she no longer trusted her ability to cope.

He'd seen flashes of doubt and insecurity in her eyes. As if she'd somehow failed. Worth had never asked why Lawrence had been going to the grocery store the night he'd died. If her husband had been running an errand for Elizabeth, she probably blamed herself for his death.

Worth couldn't fight that demon for her.

The most he could hope for was to prove to her she had the strength to fight her own demons.

Some people might think that riding a horse didn't have

much to do with life, especially Elizabeth's life which involved raising a son and getting back to climbing the corporate ladder in the hotel chain she had worked for until Jamie's birth. Worth knew better.

Successfully overcoming an ingrained fear bred success in other areas of one's life. Elizabeth felt beaten down now, but conquering her fear of horses would give her confidence in her other abilities.

His grandpa Yancy was fond of pointing out that Rome wasn't built in a day. Worth didn't expect Elizabeth to be riding Wally and roping cows before she left. Riding Rosie was nothing but a baby step toward freeing Elizabeth from a crippling fear.

Getting her on Rosie's back was a start.

If he could get her there.

CHAPTER SIX

"Mom must have dug those old jeans of Greeley's out of the rag bag, but they seem to fit okay." Worth eyed her hips as if he were measuring her for tailored trousers.

Or a shroud.

"I'm not riding a horse," Elizabeth said through her teeth. A point she'd been too stunned to make clear yesterday when Worth made his grand announcement out the back door.

"Russ thinks you are."

"Only because you told him I was. At the dinner table last night. And at breakfast this morning when you reminded your mother I needed clothes to ride in."

"Pretty clever, huh? You couldn't argue with me for fear I'd tell Russ your dirty little secret."

She couldn't believe he had the audacity to brag about his despicable behavior. "This is your idea of revenge because I refused to go along with your asinine ideas and pretend to be interested in you. I have news for you. I planned to tell you I'd play your little game, but you blew that."

"Why?"

She couldn't believe he had to ask. "Because you tried to twist my arm, that's why."

"No, why were you going to agree to play along?"

"None of your business. I've changed my mind." She wasn't about to tell him it was because he'd helped his sisters brush their teeth. "And I'm not riding any horse."

"How do you plan to get out of it?" Worth asked with great interest.

"I'm spraining my ankle," she said defiantly.

Grinning, Worth lifted a battered cowboy hat off a corral

post and plopped it on her head. "You'd better wear this. It's easy to get a sunburn at this high altitude."

Elizabeth ripped the hat from her head and flung it from her. The hat sailed into the corral and landed near the feet of the ugliest white horse she'd ever seen. A brown horse snorted in alarm and dashed to the other side of the corral, but the white horse stepped over to the hat and curiously sniffed it.

Worth pointed to the horse. "Meet Rosie. She might get excited if a fire truck snuck up behind her and blew its siren, but I doubt it."

The horse's face was long and bony, part of one ear was missing and her body was shaped like a barrel. She picked up the hat from the ground and ambled over to Worth. Up close she looked even uglier. And bigger.

Elizabeth backed away. "I'm not riding."

Worth accepted the hat from the mare. Scratching her neck, he said without looking at Elizabeth, "There are a lot of things mothers need to teach their sons. A fear of horses isn't one of them."

She sucked in air. Poor Jamie. No father and a coward for a mother. There was nothing she could do about either. "Millions of people spend their entire lives without ever going near a horse."

"They don't have Russ for a grandfather. You planning to build a wall between him and his grandson?"

"He can visit us. In a city where we don't have to ride horses." A lump grew in her throat as she thought of an older Jamie struggling to find common ground with Russ. The way she struggled.

"Russ doesn't like cities."

"I don't like horses."

Worth slapped the hat against his thigh to remove the dust and stuck it back on her head, pulling it down around her ears. Holding the brim in both hands, he drew Elizabeth toward him and said patiently, "Horses don't come any steadier than Rosie. She's intelligent and good-natured and she'll see you don't get in any trouble."

"I'm not riding," she said mechanically. Didn't he realize she would if she could?

Worth tucked a tendril of hair behind her ear. "I don't know for sure how old she is, but at least twenty-five. Hannah rides her and as soon as the babies are strong enough to sit up and hang on, they'll ride her."

Elizabeth's blood chilled. "You're not putting Jamie on her."

"I wouldn't do that. He's not ready to ride." He flicked her hat brim and walked away.

Neither was she. Elizabeth watched him open the gate to the corral, wishing she had the courage to get on the horse. Or the courage to walk away in the face of Worth's certain contempt. She put off doing anything. "Why don't you know how old the horse is?"

"Allie brought her home a few years back. This investment broker from New York, who had a second home here, was having money troubles so he let go his hired help and turned his half-dozen horses out in a small pasture. The hired couple moved away, and he stayed in New York and forgot about the horses. The horses quickly denuded the pasture and were starving to death when Allie heard about them."

"That's awful," Elizabeth said in horror.

"Three were too far gone to save." Worth led the two horses out of the corral and tied the brown one a distance from Elizabeth. "Allie managed to find homes for the other two, but this gal," he rubbed between the white horse's ears, "was old and so gaunt and bony, nobody thought she'd live, but she's got heart."

"I don't want to ride her."

"She may not look it, but Mom thinks she's part Tennessee Walker. She's got a smooth, rocking-chair gait. Blow in her nose so she'll know you're friendly."

"I'm not friendly."

"I'll fix the stirrups after you mount up."

"You're not listening to one thing I say."

"I will when you talk sense," he assured her.

The horse turned her long head to look at Elizabeth and made a small inquisitive sound.

"She has blue eyes." Only Worth Lassiter would have a blue-eyed horse.

"They're called glass eyes. Some people used to think blue-eyed horses can't see as well, but they can."

The horse had a sweet, patient face. Elizabeth worried her bottom lip indecisively. "This is stupid. Russ won't be impressed by me riding an old nag."

"You hear that, Rosie? She called you an old nag."

The horse couldn't possibly understand, but Elizabeth would swear the mare looked hurt.

"Mom sometimes rides her, but she's been knee-deep in wedding plans, so Rosie's feeling neglected. Russ thinks you're doing me a favor."

"Mary could ride her now instead of watching Jamie."

"She's involved with her wedding lists, and Jimbo's happily playing in his playpen."

"You think you've thought of everything, don't you?"

He gave her a self-satisfied grin. "Yup."

Elizabeth had a strong feeling the man and the horse would stand there all day waiting for her. She took a tentative step toward the mare. The horse barely blinked. Elizabeth took another step, and another. The horse simply watched her. Taking a deep breath, Elizabeth blew lightly into the mare's nostrils. The horse snorted gently. Elizabeth jumped back in alarm.

Worth caught her. "Ready to ride?"

"I don't know if I can," she said, hating the tremor in her voice. The next second Elizabeth found herself high above ground clutching a saddle horn while Worth adjusted her stirrups.

Then he swung aboard the brown horse. "It's like riding a bicycle. It'll all come back to you." Horse and rider headed around the barn.

Rosie stood waiting patiently for a signal from Elizabeth. She nudged the horse with her knee, and the mare ambled after

Play LUCKY HEARTS for this..

exciting FREE gift!
This surprise mystery gift could be yours free

when you play LUCKY HEARTS!

...then continue your lucky streak with a sweetheart of a deal!

1. Play Lucky Hearts as instructed on the opposite page.

2. Send back this card and you'll receive brand-new Harlequin Romance® novels. These books have a cover price of $3.50 each in the U.S. and $3.99 each in Canada, but they are yours to keep absolutely free.

3. There's no catch! You're under no obligation to buy anything. We charge nothing— ZERO—for your first shipment. And you don't have to make any minimum number of purchases—not even one!

4. The fact is thousands of readers enjoy receiving books by mail from the Harlequin Reader Service®. They enjoy the convenience of home delivery...they like getting the best new novels at discount prices, BEFORE they're available in stores...and they love their *Heart to Heart* subscriber newsletter featuring author news, horoscopes, recipes, book reviews and much more!

5. We hope that after receiving your free books you'll want to remain a subscriber. But the choice is yours—to continue or cancel, any time at all! So why not take us up on our invitation, with no risk of any kind. You'll be glad you did!

◆ Exciting Harlequin romance novels—FREE!
◆ Plus an exciting mystery gift—FREE!

◆ DETACH AND MAIL CARD TODAY!

The Harlequin Reader Service®—Here's how it works:

Accepting your 2 free books and gift places you under no obligation to buy anything. You may keep the books and gift and return the shipping statement marked "cancel." If you do not cancel, about a month later we'll send you 6 additional novels and bill you just $2.90 each in the U.S., or $3.34 each in Canada, plus 25¢ delivery per book and applicable taxes if any.* That's the complete price and — compared to cover prices of $3.50 each in the U.S. and $3.99 each in Canada — it's quite a bargain! You may cancel at any time, but if you choose to continue, every month we'll send you 6 more books, which you may either purchase at the discount price or return to us and cancel your subscription.

*Terms and prices subject to change without notice. Sales tax applicable in N.Y. Canadian residents will be charged applicable provincial taxes and GST.

Worth. He didn't bother to look back but led the way across an empty pasture.

The mare walked with a smooth, even gait and Elizabeth gradually relaxed enough to notice her surroundings. A jet contrail drew a line in the brilliant blue sky above white-tipped mountain peaks. As they entered a meadow, a deer on the other side raised its head, then bounded into the trees and disappeared. Worth followed a track through the grass. Hearing a faint rustle over the sound of horse hooves, Elizabeth looked down to see a ground squirrel frozen beneath the leaves of a wild geranium. Her breath caught as she waited for Rosie to bolt, but the mare merely noted the small mammal, then placidly walked on. Elizabeth expelled air with a whoosh of relief.

After about thirty minutes Worth stopped his horse on top of a small knoll and waited for Elizabeth to join him. Silently he pointed to a small stock pond below. A female mallard floated on the water's surface, seemingly ignoring the balls of fluff paddling behind her.

Worth rested his forearms on the saddle horn. "Why'd you come?"

"At which point did you give me a choice?" she asked tartly.

"I thought you were going to fake a sprained ankle."

"A lot you would have cared if I had sprained my ankle."

He gave her a lazy smile, not acknowledging her charge. "You know I wouldn't have forced you to ride."

"I knew you'd bully me until I did exactly what you wanted me to do, so it seemed a lot easier to get it over with."

"You need to learn how to control your blushes if you're going to go around telling whopping lies, Red. That's not why you're riding. Miss being on a horse, did you?"

"No." Overhead a swallow swooped low to snatch a bit of cotton drifting from a cottonwood tree. Elizabeth fiddled with the leather reins. "Did your sisters ever manage to keep anything from you?"

He screwed up his face as if he was giving her question serious thought. After a few seconds he grinned. "Nope. So you might as well fess up and tell me the real reason why you're riding. You know I'll bully you until you do,'' he added with dry amusement.

Elizabeth had no intention of telling him anything. Her reasons for riding were none of his business. "Why is she named Rosie?"

"We never knew her name." Worth straightened. "We can ride side by side here." Their horses moved off. "She was so thin, she was lumpy when Allie showed up with her. The hands wanted to name her Mashed Potatoes and call her Spud, but she'd been subjected to enough indignities. Her coat was filthy from rolling in red mud, so I named her Rosie."

Worth continued to surprise her with unexpected sides to his personality. His complexities made it difficult to pigeonhole him. Or ignore him. She slanted a look at him from under her hat. "Have you ever been scared of anything in your life?"

"Sure."

"Name something."

He rubbed the bridge of his nose with a gloved hand. "When I was about eleven, I overheard a conversation in a store about a couple being killed in a car accident and leaving behind a bunch of kids. One lady said the kids were split up because no one wanted to take them all. I was scared to death Mom and Grandpa would die on us. Cheyenne was five, Allie four and Greeley about Jimbo's age. I spent weeks planning how we'd run away and hide so nobody could split us up. Mom found out when she went riding one day and came across my stash of canned goods in an old line shack."

"Was she mad?"

"Annoyed I'd tried to solve the problem on my own instead of going to her. Turned out she and Zane's folks had put in their wills that each would take care of the other's kids if something happened to them. As soon as I was legally old enough, she arranged that I'd be my sisters' guardian if anything happened to her."

Elizabeth focused on Rosie's tattered ear. "So the last time you were scared of anything, you were still a boy."

Worth reined in his horse. "Every year I'm scared the alfalfa will get hailed out, that we'll lose calves in a late spring blizzard, or a mare'll have trouble foaling."

"I'm not talking about those kinds of fears," she said impatiently. "I mean being afraid of the dark or heights or spiders. That kind of thing."

Leaning forward, he rubbed his horse's neck. A pair of pale peach-colored butterflies played tag over the meadow. The drowsy silence was broken by a staccato drumming sound as a flicker searched for bugs near the top of a blue spruce tree. Worth's horse stamped its foot, and the bird flew away with a flash of russet feathers. Worth didn't answer her question. Probably because there wasn't anything which scared him.

Elizabeth studied a low area filled with faded iris and wondered why they didn't move on.

"It scares me half to death that I'll turn out to be like Beau," Worth said unexpectedly in a voice so quiet Elizabeth could barely hear him. "The family's always condemned Greeley's birth mother for walking away from her baby, but we don't talk much about how our father abandoned his entire family. We made excuses for him, but the truth is, he was a cold-hearted, selfish man who used Mom and had no interest in his offspring." The deliberate lack of emotion in his voice gave his words the unmistakable ring of truth.

Elizabeth knew how ridiculous his fear was, but she also understood how real it was to him. Logic had nothing to do with fear.

No one knew that better than she. Fear had become her constant companion. She hated it, but hating didn't make it go away.

Impulsively she reached over and laid her hand over his as it rested on his thigh. "You may be a lot of things, Worth Lassiter, including arrogant, single-minded, obnoxious, and a bully, but you would never abandon your family. I didn't know your father, but I haven't heard anything about him that tells me you're like him."

He lifted her hand from his and played with her fingers. "Gotcha, didn't I?"

Elizabeth stiffened with indignation, but before she could lash out at him, she noticed the tiny muscle jumping in his jaw. Worth was trying to pass his confession off as a joke. Baring his soul had obviously embarrassed him. An endearing, little-boy trait. Hanging on to his hand for support, she stood in her stirrups and, leaning over, planted a kiss on his cheek.

Her hat collided with his, knocking both to the ground. Worth touched his cheek and gave her a whimsical smile. "I'll have to remember that line the next time I want a pretty girl to kiss me." Bending down, he swept their hats up off the ground.

Elizabeth wasn't about to let him think she was so stupid she couldn't tell the difference between truth and malarkey. "If you are so desperate that you're making up pathetic nonsense to attract women, your sisters are right. You need to get married now. As soon as we get back, I'm calling Cheyenne and telling her I'll be happy to help her find you a wife."

"You are one mean woman, Red."

Elizabeth just laughed and put her hat back on.

They'd circled around and were approaching the house from a different direction. A riot of colorful wildflowers caught her eye. A rusted wrought-iron fence enclosed a small garden. She hadn't seen it before. "What is that?"

Worth followed her gaze. "Sort of a memorial garden. The house is through those cottonwoods. If you want to look around, you can walk from here. I'll take care of Rosie."

Elizabeth wouldn't win any prizes for horsemanship, but Russ had taught her the rudiments of riding. Cautiously she climbed down from the mare, hoping Rosie wouldn't bolt for the barn. The mare yawned.

Worth smiled. "Congratulations. You survived."

"Yes." She handed him Rosie's reins.

"I thought you might come down to the corral, give me a piece of your mind for pushing you to ride, and then walk away. Why didn't you, Red? Tell me the truth this time. I didn't force you to walk up to Rosie, to blow in her nostrils.''

''You threw me on her.''

''You just proved you can get off all by yourself. But you didn't at the corral? Going to tell me why?''

''No. I'm not sure I can explain it.'' She stared at the stitching on his jean-clad thigh. ''I used to fear nothing. Except horses. But since Lawrence died… It's insidious, fear. Before you know it, it rules your life. Becomes a prison. I was doing that to myself. Locking myself in a prison of fear. What you said about Jamie…''

A bee buzzed past. Demonstrating what she'd lacked for the past year. A purpose. ''I can't raise him to be afraid of every little shadow. But I didn't ride Rosie just for Jamie's sake. I rode her for me.''

Elizabeth stuck her hands in her back pockets. ''If a person runs away from fear, fear wins. I haven't been fighting fear; I've been conceding. Letting what happened beat me.'' She looked up into Worth's shadowed face. ''When I came here I felt sorry for myself. I told myself you all were lucky because you'd never known what it was to suffer. I was wrong. Everyone has rough spots in their lives. You all fight back. It's time I started fighting back, too.''

Without waiting for a response, Elizabeth made a wide berth around the horses and headed for the gate in the fence.

A path of flat concrete stones wound through a cottage garden of wild blooms. Leaning over, she made out words scratched in the concrete. Names and dates. Taking care not to step on pale pink wild roses or bright blue harebells, Elizabeth followed the path, reading the inscriptions as she went. Teddy. Black Bart. Meow Meow. The names must belong to family pets. Older stones suggested the garden had served many generations.

The gate clanked as Worth joined her.

''You've had so many pets,'' she said.

''I think Allie started bringing home unwanted and abused animals before she could walk. Most of them we never knew

when they were born, so we recorded the day they came to the
Double Nickel. Some of them were so bad off, they weren't
with us long, but hopefully, their last days were better than
what went before. We usually took in the ones no one else
wanted."

Elizabeth peered more closely at the dates on the stones. She
knew his sister had gone away to school and worked in Denver
before she married. There was no cessation of animals during
that time. Allie obviously knew one person she could count on
to never turn away an animal, no matter how old or sick or
ugly.

A gray-striped female cat was currently in residence. Hannah
had explained to Elizabeth that she and Allie had given the
abandoned kitten to Mary. Elizabeth noticed the cat spent most
of her time in Worth's office and that Worth never failed to
pet or speak to the animal in passing.

Worth leaned down and brushed off a stone inscribed with
the name Shadow. "He was a good ol' dog. Deaf, blind, lame,
but I kind of got used to having him around. He had a lot of
heart."

A lot of heart. Like Rosie. Like Worth.

She concentrated on a clump of columbine.

"Allie's been after me to take another dog, but so far I've
managed to put her off."

Movement caught Elizabeth's eye. A bluebird with a large
insect in his mouth flew past and landed on an old birdhouse
at the other side of the garden. A second bird, gray with tinges
of blue, landed beside him, and the male fed the bug to the
female.

She'd read male bluebirds helped raise their families.

Easy to guess why Worth didn't want another dog. "I suppose it might be a little difficult to walk a dog on the Great
Wall of China."

He gave her a slight smile.

He didn't deny it.

Elizabeth thought about him at age eleven preparing to take
care of his sisters in case of an emergency. An eleven-year-

old shouldn't have to worry about becoming the head of a family. If ever there was a person who deserved a time to be footloose and fancy-free, to explore new horizons, that person was Worth Lassiter.

"All right," she said abruptly. "I'll do it."

If he wasn't behind the wheel as they drove to the jazz festival, Worth would be watching Elizabeth. And trying to figure out what Allie's hairdresser had done to Elizabeth's hair. He hadn't been happy about her going to the beauty shop with his mother, but nobody asked his opinion. He'd half expected Elizabeth to return with short, chopped-off hair like Allie's.

Her red hair didn't look any shorter, except maybe around her face, but it was definitely different. Her eyes looked greener, her face fuller, more expressive. Sexier.

Living with three sisters and a mother, all with totally different personalities, he'd thought he knew all there was to know about women. In his family, each woman could be counted on to react predictably to a given situation. Elizabeth reacted in ten different ways in as many minutes.

Worth wondered how Lawrence Randall had managed to live for a year with such a mercurial, contradictory woman. Being married to her must have been like riding a roller coaster. Steady ascents, breathless heights and moments of sheer panic when you wondered where she'd take you next.

Worth wasn't about to push his luck and ask Elizabeth why she'd agreed to his arrangement. If she couldn't come up with solid reasons, she was as likely as not to change her mind.

"Nobody's going to believe you're seriously interested in me when you could have your pick of starlets and socialites."

"Is that supposed to be a compliment?"

She didn't crack a smile. "I'm widowed, have a child and I don't like horses."

"Nobody knows that part." He added smoothly, "That's the crux of our arrangement. We pretend we have a growing attachment to each other, and I not only keep secret your dislike of horses, I provide you with excuses for not riding."

Not that the arrangement mattered any more. Even Cheyenne couldn't entangle him with a woman in the few days left before the wedding. The time he'd spent with Elizabeth convinced him she hadn't come to sabotage the wedding, so he no longer needed to keep her occupied and away from Russ.

The truth was, he'd kept after her about it more for the challenge than anything else. And to annoy her. Sparring with him gave her something to think about besides her bereavement.

Plus, he didn't mind an opportunity to give Cheyenne a strong message that she should mind her own business.

"Your sisters will immediately guess you're pretending to like me because you don't want them matchmaking. I'll look like a fool."

"They'll assume they know my motives. What will have them guessing is yours. I told you, make me the villain. They'll have no problem believing I'm forcing you to fake an interest in me." He smiled encouragingly across the width of the pickup. "You don't look like a fool. You look good."

"Good," Elizabeth echoed in disgust. "Is that like, hey, that steak looks good?"

Worth gave her solemn look. "To a rancher, there's nothing better-looking than a steak."

She made a face, but said nothing more, content to watch the passing scenery.

She'd made fun of the word, but she did look good. The sun had replaced her wan pallor with a faint pink, and her eyes were no longer sunk in dark pockets. She was eating and sleeping better.

She laughed easier.

Being here agreed with Jamie, too. He'd quit shrinking from Russ's gruff voice, and grew in boldness as he explored the ranch house. After catching him eying the stairs, Worth had installed child safety gates at the top and the bottom.

Elizabeth's voice broke into his thoughts. "How do you know Jake Norton and his wife so well?"

"Some years ago Jake filmed a Western movie in the area

and he stayed with us to learn about ranching and get in character. You and he have a lot in common. He hates horses, too.''

"Jake Norton hates horses? He's one of the biggest Western heroes around. I thought he was born and raised on a ranch.''

"Hollywood hype. He comes from a small town in Iowa. Don't tell him I gave away his big secret.''

"Why did you? I could sell it to the tabloids and make a bundle.''

"It's one of the worst-kept secrets in Hollywood. Besides,'' he leered outrageously at her, "we're supposed to be a couple, remember? We trust each other with secrets. That's what couples do.''

Her face totally froze.

Worth mentally cursed himself for reminding her she was no longer part of a couple. Hoping to divert her thoughts, he launched into a history lesson about the beginnings of Aspen.

Elizabeth barely listened as Worth discoursed about mining and Ute Indians and skiing and cultural centers. He might know tons of things about Aspen, but he knew nothing about marriage. Couples didn't always trust each other. At least, not both halves of a couple. She'd blindly trusted Lawrence. He'd abused that trust so vilely it sickened her to think about it. But she couldn't put it from her mind. It was as if certain words were engraved deep down in the center of her brain. Lawrence hates Elizabeth. Lawrence hates Elizabeth. The refrain echoed over and over again like a mean, childish, playground taunt.

"You need a little practice.''

"What?'' Worth's words jerked her from black memories.

"You're supposed to be hanging on my every word,'' he said patiently, "not having your mind somewhere out in the ozone.''

"I was. Listening, I mean. Somebody named Meeker killed Indians on Independence Day during a snowstorm.''

"Meeker was killed by Indians a hundred miles from here, nowhere near Independence Pass, which was the route miners took to reach Aspen from Leadville. Some of the first came through more than five feet of snow.'' He abruptly switched subjects. ''I'm telling you, you don't have a thing to worry about tonight.''

Elizabeth shut down thoughts of Lawrence's treachery before Worth guessed her preoccupation had nothing to do with this evening. She ought to be terrified about going to a jazz concert with a group which included one of Hollywood's brightest stars and the head of an exclusive hotel chain she'd give her eyeteeth to work for. Not to mention she'd agreed to participate in a farce which no one would believe. She'd look like an idiot.

She fought an impulse to giggle, probably from rising hysteria. ''I can't believe I agreed to do this. Riding Rosie must have scrambled my brain.''

''That's what happens when you ride a bucking bronco,'' Worth said solemnly. Warm laughter danced in his eyes.

No one ever told her you could drown in blue eyes.

For one crazy second the world tilted crazily on its axis.

Elizabeth wanted him to kiss her. It was absolutely insane, but she wanted him to stop the truck, take her in his arms, and cover her face with kisses.

''This is Snowmass. We'll have to walk from here.''

Blinking out of her trance, Elizabeth looked around. Worth had parked the pickup and was getting out. In front of them a small stream of people headed up a slight incline. Worth opened her door and she stepped down.

Most of the people carried heavy coats and blankets. One woman wore what looked like a silk trouser suit and another wore a skimpy knit camisole with a long skirt almost completely unbuttoned in front. Elizabeth shivered just looking at the scantily clad woman.

''Cold already?''

She shook her head. ''Your mother insisted I wear her silk long underwear under my jeans. I feel guilty dumping Jamie on her again. I could have stayed home or brought him.''

''Mom's happy to have the excuse not to come. She says she's too old for outdoor concerts and Russ doesn't like jazz.

My baby nieces won't be here either.'' He handed her their coats and grabbed the blankets behind his seat and two low folding chairs from the back of the truck.

Towering mountains were beginning to shadow this end of the alpine valley. The Nortons, Steeles, Peters and Damians had already staked out a spot in front of a huge white tent in the large field. Hannah saw Elizabeth and Worth and jumped up, waving her arms and yelling at them. Elizabeth was too loaded down to wave back, but she smiled and nodded. Hannah and Davy raced toward them.

Worth bent to speak in her ear. ''You'll notice where they chose to sit.''

A half-dozen young women sprawled near the Lassiter family group. Elizabeth saw absolutely no sign either group knew the other. She laughed up into Worth's face. ''Talk about paranoia. I'll bet your sisters haven't even noticed who's beside them.''

Worth kissed her on the mouth.

Elizabeth forgot everything but the feel of his lips against hers.

He raised his head, satisfaction gleaming in his eyes. ''I'm going to enjoy this.'' He slanted his eyes toward his family.

Elizabeth followed his gaze and swallowed hard. The expressions on the faces of the group waiting for them ran the gamut from interest through surprise to shock. Except for Thomas Steele who looked amused.

Davy, reaching them, took the chairs from Worth, so Hannah insisted on carrying Elizabeth's coat. Nerves jangled in Elizabeth's stomach, but everyone greeted them with a friendly welcome. By the time she'd returned greetings and arranged their blankets and chairs, Elizabeth had managed to bring her racing pulse under control.

Worth had taken her by surprise. If he'd warned her, she wouldn't have... Wouldn't have what? Kissed him back so enthusiastically? Been tempted to burrow into his body?

Or forgotten they played a game of pretend?

Cheyenne brought it up first. Davy and the men had wandered off to collect dinner from the various booths decorating the perimeter of the field. Kristy and Greeley went with Hannah to where portable toilets had been set up. "About Worth kissing you..." Cheyenne began.

Elizabeth felt the blush heating her face and busied herself refolding the coat she'd borrowed from Mary. "Well, you know how, uh, he is."

Cheyenne sighed. "I know exactly how he is. I'm not sure how to say this..." She looked at Allie.

"You started it," her sister said.

"Don't take me wrong, Elizabeth. That is, I don't want you to, I mean..." She gestured aimlessly.

"I know he's using me as a shield against other women," Elizabeth said before Cheyenne could warn her away from Worth.

"I suppose he could be, partly," Allie said. "Mostly he's using you to teach Cheyenne a lesson. No reason you should let him."

This was the tricky part. "We're sort of scratching each other's backs, if you know what I mean?"

A dead silence greeted her question, then Cheyenne gave her an arrested look. "He's blackmailing you?" she asked in an outraged voice.

"I didn't say that."

"You don't have to. I know Worth and his tricks. I can't believe he'd pull that on you. How in the world did he learn something you didn't... Never mind. Do you enjoy jazz? I adore these concerts as much for the ambiance as the music. You can buy tickets for inside the tent or out here. It gets colder out here, but it's more fun, especially with the kids. We can watch the concert on the big TVs they've set up." She pointed to one. "The sound out here is just as great."

Later, Allie walked with Elizabeth to the toilets. "When it comes to your deep, dark secrets, you can trust Worth absolutely. He's safer than a bank vault." Allie hesitated. "And if it's something you need help with, you can count on Worth."

Elizabeth had no intention of trusting anyone, including Worth, with her deepest, darkest secret.

Worth shifted a sleeping Hannah to a more comfortable spot on his lap. Even in the dark he saw the quick smile Elizabeth flashed him as she rearranged Hannah's legs. Hannah had insisted on sitting on both their laps so they'd put their armless chairs as close together as they could, and shared the blankets, one behind them and one draped over Hannah and their laps. With the exception of Allie and Zane cuddled together in a cluster of blankets, the other couples were paired off in chairs. Davy's nose peeked out of a sleeping bag near Thomas's chair.

The Nortons, Worth's sisters and their spouses, exemplified the best kinds of married couples. They worked hard at keeping their marriages strong.

And enjoyed the rewards.

Envy surged out of nowhere, surprising Worth. How could he envy them? Zane, Quint, Thomas, even Jake—they were all tied down, tied to each other, tied to their children.

Heartstrings, his mother called them. Love tied you to people. That was fine if a man wanted to be tied down.

A man couldn't pat a wife and child on their heads and take off for weeks at a time to indulge his own selfish interests. A husband, a father, had to be there for his family.

Beau had never been there for them. Worth didn't want his kids feeling about him the way Worth felt about his father.

Someday he wanted marriage, a wife, children. Heartstrings. Someday. Not now. Not yet. There was a whole world out there waiting to be explored. He didn't want to be tied down until he'd seen at least some of it.

Elizabeth's thigh bumped rhythmically against him as she tapped her foot to the beat. He was conscious of her breathing, heard her little sounds of pleasure in the musical performance.

He wished they were wrapped in each other's arms on the ground, wearing nothing but the blankets.

That's what came of kissing her.

The improvisational wail of a single saxophone faded away,

the last haunting notes lingering on the night air. Elizabeth sighed with quiet contentment. "Beautiful." She tipped back her head. "Look how bright the stars are."

He'd rather look at her, but he obediently looked up. The Big Dipper and Arcturus shone brilliantly in a crystal clear night sky. Worth searched for and found the twin stars of Gemini. Once he'd wanted to be an astronaut. Go to the moon, travel in space.

Be released from earth's gravity.

There'd been times in his late teens and early twenties when he'd felt as if the entire gravity of earth pulled at him alone. Times when he'd been so afraid his sisters would realize the older brother they depended on to be a sturdy oak tree was only an insubstantial twig.

The final number, played with a swinging rhythm and fresh, spontaneous beat, met with a burst of applause, and the concert ended. Around them people packed up coats and blankets and streamed toward the parking lots. Zane collected Hannah, and Davy struggled sleepily out of the sleeping bag. Everyone said quiet goodbyes, then, hand in hand, his sisters and their husbands and children joined the homeward-bound crowd.

Worth and Elizabeth followed. Ahead of them Quint pulled Greeley close and whispered in her ear. Her soft laughter floated back to Worth as the couple stopped and kissed.

"You're not newlyweds anymore," Worth grumbled as he walked around them. "Can't you wait until you get back to Cheyenne's?"

"You're just jealous," Greeley said, abandoning Quint to press a kiss on her brother's cheek.

He wasn't jealous.

Maybe it would be nice to go home and crawl into bed with Elizabeth. It wasn't going to happen.

He'd admit to an inconvenient physical attraction to a certain redheaded woman. It was nothing more than a temporary loss of sanity. It would pass.

When he married, when his traveling days were over, he planned to marry a woman like his mother. Calm, levelheaded,

and easygoing. Mary took life in her stride. Not in a million
years could he picture his mother standing in the middle of
someone else's kitchen wearing sexy green pajamas and yelling at a man she barely knew.

Mary would fight like a tiger for her kids, but Worth was
pretty sure she'd never owned a pair of green pajamas.

CHAPTER SEVEN

THE pickup's twin beams pierced the dark as they drove back to the ranch. Catching a glimpse of the Roaring Fork River between the trees, Elizabeth imagined starlight dancing on the rapids. She hugged the beauty to her, wishing she could box it up and take it back to Nebraska with her.

She knew it wasn't the scenery she wanted to keep forever. What she would sorely miss was being part of the Lassiter family circle. They'd welcomed Elizabeth into their midst, making her feel as if she belonged, even if it was to be only for these two short weeks.

Back in Nebraska her empty house waited. Silent. Filled not with love and laughter, but with painful memories.

They'd bought the house shortly after they'd married. Lawrence had initially been against the move, had wanted them to stay in his apartment, but Elizabeth persuaded him that buying a house was a better investment than renting.

If Lawrence hadn't hated finances and budget details and paperwork so much, if he hadn't trusted Elizabeth so much, he wouldn't have allowed her to handle the financial side of their marriage. He would have known if one died, the additional insurance she'd purchased paid the mortgage so that the house belonged free and clear to the survivor.

Lawrence hadn't expected to die.

After his death everyone told Elizabeth she'd been wise to get the additional insurance. She hadn't told them it was the only smart thing she'd done when it came to her marriage.

Now the house seemed a trap. A sinkhole of apathy and depression and failure.

She didn't have to stay there.

She could sell the house. Or change it. Paint it inside and

112

out. Make it her and Jamie's home. Remove any trace of Lawrence.

Maybe Mary could tell her where to buy cowboy posters for the walls in Jamie's room. She stiffened her spine. She and Jamie would manage just fine.

"Did you enjoy the evening?"

Worth's question provided a welcome distraction from her thoughts. "You're lucky to have such a close-knit family. Zane told me tonight your mother used to barrel race and that's how she met his mother."

Worth nodded. "Zane and I grew up together. We even cut ourselves one time and mixed our blood so we could be blood brothers. We saw it on TV or something."

"And now he's married to your sister."

"For his sins," Worth said lightly.

"He told me about those, too. How he messed up with Hannah's mother and left Allie practically standing at the altar." She hesitated. "Did you really cut him out of your life for five years?"

"Yes."

The clipped answer told Elizabeth a great deal. "It must have been painful for you. Losing your best friend that way."

"Allie's my sister."

The simple, uncompromising statement spoke volumes about the depth of Worth's family loyalty. Zane claimed Worth was the kind of man who would die for his family. No wonder Worth's sisters concerned themselves with his happiness. They knew he'd been there for them. They wanted to return the favor.

Even if they were wrong about what Worth needed.

She gave Worth a quick glance. "Your sisters are not happy with you."

"I saw Cheyenne and Allie pounce on you while I was buying dinner. I'll bet Cheyenne is gnashing her teeth in frustration about how I outsmarted her."

"I wouldn't exactly say that."

Worth gave a long, resigned sigh. "What's on their pea

brains now? You might as well tell me what they're planning. I'll find out sooner or later.''

''It's not so much what they're planning...'' She let the end of the sentence fade away, deliberately teasing him.

After a few minutes, Worth said in a brooding voice, ''That smug note in your voice makes me nervous.''

''You've never been nervous in your life.''

''You make me nervous.''

''I'll have you know, Worth Lassiter, I am just as good as you at keeping secrets. I didn't say one word to your sisters about why you don't want to get married now.''

''I didn't say you did.''

''You said I make you nervous. What else could you possibly mean except you're worried I'll give away your big secret?'' Turning her back to him, Elizabeth stared out the window, angry he didn't trust her. She could feel him looking at her.

''Green pajamas,'' he said at last.

She whipped her head around. ''Green pajamas?''

''You look too good in green pajamas. I start wondering how you look out of them and that makes me real nervous. I've never had any trouble resisting forbidden fruit before.''

He wanted to sleep with her? He couldn't possibly want to sleep with her. ''I'm puny. You called me puny.'' To her chagrin, her voice squeaked on the last word.

A crooked smile bent his mouth. ''Unfortunately for me, puny and sexy as all get-out are not mutually exclusive.''

''You think I'm sexy?''

''You have a mirror. It can't come as a revelation.''

No one had ever called her sexy. She knew she cleaned up well, and she'd heard herself referred to as attractive and nice-looking, but never sexy. Worth Lassiter, considered by his sisters to be the world's most eligible bachelor, thought her sexy? It was crazy.

Common sense called a halt to her vain and foolish thoughts before she could totally humiliate herself.

Worth no more thought she was sexy than he thought she was the cowboy Russ bragged she was. ''You need to be a little more careful with your joking,'' she said, ''or some woman who doesn't know you as well as I do will believe you, and you'll be a married man before you know what hit you. Your sisters won't need to find you a wife.''

The cool night seeped through the pickup's windows, chilling Elizabeth. Stretching her feet under the heater in search of its paltry output of warmth, she huddled deeper into Mary's coat. A rabbit showed its terrorized face in the truck's headlights, froze momentarily, then abruptly turned and bounded away from the road.

Worth cleared his throat. ''You never told me what Cheyenne had to say.''

Elizabeth had spent the evening anticipating the moment she'd tell him what she'd learned. For whatever reason, the tale no longer seemed so amusing. ''You were right about them immediately assuming you couldn't possibly be interested in me.''

''I don't think I ever said that.''

His exact words weren't worth debating. Not when everyone agreed on the absurdity of coupling Elizabeth with him. ''As you expected, they concluded you're trying to teach Cheyenne a lesson. As instructed, when asked why I was cooperating, I hinted at blackmail, and they dropped it.''

''And?''

''It was just interesting, the way they positively leaped, with hardly any help from me, to the conclusion that you were blackmailing me.'' She paused, but he didn't admit anything, so she continued. ''Apparently, it was quite an easy conclusion for them to reach. Based on your past history and fondness for blackmail.''

Worth made a disgusted sound. ''Let me tell you something, Red. I have three sisters with more hair than brains. I used whatever worked to keep them in line.'' After a minute, he added brusquely, ''No matter what they accused me of, I only used blackmail as a last resort. And it worked.''

His confidence in his own judgment was as arrogant as it was unwarranted. ''Allie said by the time they were in high school they knew you'd never go through with your blackmail, no matter what you threatened, because you'd never hurt them.''

"They talk big now, but let me tell you, they shaped right up then," he said with satisfaction.

It was a pleasure to set him straight. "So I understand. It seems Cheyenne had read some psychology book, and based on that, she said it would be bad for your self-esteem if they let you know they considered your blackmail empty threats. So they buckled under for your own good." Elizabeth waited for him to take offense and insist she'd heard wrong or his sisters had lied to her.

Worth's deep laughter filled the pickup. When his last chuckles died away, he shook his head. "Sisters."

A woman could learn to love a man who knew how to laugh at himself.

Worth could take a joke as well as the next man, but Cheyenne was carrying this foolishness too far. He scowled across the Peters' yard at Cheyenne and Elizabeth. The significance of half a dozen unattached males at the barbecue Zane and Allie were hosting for the bridal couple hadn't hit him at first. He got the picture about the time Cheyenne had hauled the third sucker over to Elizabeth for an introduction.

He wondered cynically if Cheyenne touted Elizabeth as an eligible widow or if his sister was trying to be subtle. Subtlety wasn't exactly her strong suit. The men were so busy drooling over Elizabeth's red hair and trim curves, they probably hadn't realized Cheyenne was baiting a marital trap for one of them. With Elizabeth as bait. There was nothing like green eyes to shut down a man's brain.

Which was fine with him. Elizabeth needed a husband and Jamie needed a father.

At least finding Elizabeth a husband diverted Cheyenne's attention from Worth.

He frowned. That part bothered him. It wasn't like Cheyenne to give up so easily when she was convinced she was right.

Maybe she could only handle one difficult challenge at a time. Finding Elizabeth a decent husband wasn't going to be easy. Not if these were the best candidates Cheyenne could dig up. Worth knew most of them. Nice enough men, but not men who would interest Elizabeth.

Like the man who'd just driven up. He managed a bar. And had to be at least a year younger than Elizabeth. She already had one kid to take care of.

Cheyenne immediately captured the poor sap and dragged him to Elizabeth's side. Worth caught Zane's eye. His brother-in-law smirked at him from by the barbecue grill. Which meant Allie knew about Cheyenne's plan, and was probably actively supporting it. Couldn't any of these men control their wives?

Worth had had enough. Somebody had to save Elizabeth from Cheyenne's clutches, and apparently no one else had the good sense to stop his out-of-control sister. Cheyenne ought to have better sense. Elizabeth had been a widow for barely more than a year. She wasn't interested in finding another husband.

Stalking over to the group of three, Worth muttered a greeting to the baby-faced bartender and said, "Jimbo wants his mother." He took Elizabeth's arm in a firm grip and hauled her away.

He didn't care if they all knew it was a lie. The last time he'd seen Jamie, the little boy had been happily playing with the other children under the watchful gaze of several women.

"I apologize for my sister's bad taste," he said tersely, stopping out of everyone else's earshot.

Elizabeth gave him an amused look. "What's so bad about it? I think the lawyer's awfully good-looking. He's divorced, but he keeps in very close contact with his daughter. He loves kids."

Worth snorted in disgust. "He lives in Aspen and his daughter lives in Chicago and he sees her maybe one week a year. He actually told you he loves kids?"

"Of course not. Cheyenne did."

"I used to give my sister credit for having some smarts," he said grimly.

"The gentleman who works for Thomas is fascinating," Elizabeth continued, as if Worth had any interest whatsoever in the man. "Thomas has two hotels in New York City, and that man is next in line to manage the small, intimate one on Central Park. Your rancher friend is very nice, but all he talks about is horses.''

''It is unbelievably insensitive of my sister to shove eligible bachelors down your throat before you are ready. If anything happened to Thomas, she'd shoot anyone who suggested what she needed was a husband to take his place.''

Elizabeth stared at him. ''You think Cheyenne's trying to find me a husband?'' Her voice rang with astonishment.

''Welcome to the family,'' he said ungraciously, annoyed with her failure to recognize Cheyenne's heavy-handed match-making. Jamie could have figured out what was going on. ''She's finally accepted I'm off-limits, and she's married off her sisters, so you're all that's left.''

Elizabeth dissolved into laughter. Worth saw nothing humorous about the situation. He glared at her. Which caused her to laugh harder. Crossing his arms in front of his chest, he waited.

The fact that he wasn't laughing with her finally penetrated Elizabeth's thick skull. ''Not me,'' she gasped. ''You.''

''Don't be an idiot. She hasn't introduced me to a single woman this afternoon.''

Elizabeth hiccupped. ''That's because she's coming at you from a different direction.''

''You're talking hogwash.''

She shook her head, her eyes brimming with silent laughter. ''I can't believe you didn't see it coming. It's brilliant.''

Worth gave her a blank look.

''She started by putting eligible women your way. You countered with me. She told me you were using me. You blocked that move by having me admit to being blackmailed. After thinking that over, since she's not the least bit worried you'll actually carry out whatever threats you've made to me, she's bombarding me with men.''

Elizabeth's patient explanation which explained nothing set his teeth on edge. ''Exactly how did you reach the ridiculous conclusion that her fixing you up has anything to do with me?''

''Don't you get it? If she finds someone for me, you'll have to quit pretending you're already taken. Even if she doesn't find someone, she hopes to distract and entertain me. Either way, you'll be left defenseless. You have to admit, it's a masterful plan. No wonder Cheyenne scares you. She's a genius.''

Perhaps she'd gone a little far with her praise. The way Worth's mouth thinned with annoyance suggested he didn't share Elizabeth's admiration of Cheyenne's strategy. He frowned across the yard at his sister, then turned back to Elizabeth, a thoughtful expression on his face. ''You're close, but wrong. Cheyenne isn't trying to get you out of the way. In her own convoluted way of thinking, she's decided I'm interested in you, but I don't know it. So she's giving me a helpful little shove, trying to make me jealous.'' His eyes narrowed. ''I think my sister the meddler has just played right into my hands.''

Not liking the way he appeared to be assessing her, Elizabeth shook her head. ''I don't know what you have in mind, but the answer is definitely no.''

''We have a deal,'' he reminded her softly.

''I think I'm changing my mind about that.''

''And break my sister's heart? I don't think so.'' He smiled tenderly at Elizabeth. ''You shouldn't be out here without a hat. You'll burn.'' He trailed a thumb along the top of her cheekbone.

His sudden concern for her welfare made her nervous. And stole the stiffening from her knees. ''I'm okay,'' she said breathlessly. ''I'll just go sit on the porch in the shade. In a little while.'' Her legs refused to obey her command to walk away. She couldn't move.

Not if he was planning to kiss her.

Worth slid his hand over her shoulder, then pulled her arm around his waist and tucked her snugly against him. The day's heat lingering in the ranch yard felt cool compared to the warmth radiating from his body.

Elizabeth knew without a doubt he wanted her. His desire sizzled between them.

Then he smiled into her eyes, and an astonishing discovery

sent her stomach zipping to her toes. More than lusting after her body, Worth Lassiter cared about her.

Elizabeth waited for uneasiness or dread to trickle down her spine.

Oddly enough, her heart wanted to fly. Squeezing Worth's waist, she returned his smile and lifted her face.

He bent his head and pressed a light kiss on the corner of her mouth. "Keep looking at me like that," he said against her lips. "You're very convincing."

"I assume Jamie is fine."

Elizabeth jumped as Cheyenne's sarcastic comment came from behind her. Worth's grip tightened. Elizabeth thought she might be sick. She'd totally misinterpreted his behavior. There had been nothing caring or genuine about the look in his eyes or the kiss he'd given her. He'd seen Cheyenne coming and been acting for her benefit.

Worth gave his sister an easy grin. "Turns out he didn't want his mom after all."

As if she were standing outside her body watching a play, Elizabeth saw herself smile at Cheyenne and the bachelor she had in tow. Behind them the setting sun spiked the western sky with yellow.

How stupid she was. Allowing herself to think, even for a split second... Ruthlessly she slammed the door on the thought before she could complete it and turned her attention back to Worth and Cheyenne.

Cheyenne spoke first, in a challenging voice. "I wanted Elizabeth to meet the fitness expert at St. Chris's new health club."

The tall, muscled, blond Greek god beside Worth's sister flashed a dazzling smile at Elizabeth. Worth slid his hand down to spread his fingers possessively over Elizabeth's hip. The Greek god's gaze flew straight to Worth's hand. Elizabeth pinched Worth's waist hard. He didn't even flinch. The Greek god looked at Elizabeth's hair, took a second look at Worth's hand, gave a lopsided smile and took a polite leave of them.

"I don't know what hole you're dragging all these men out of, Cheyenne, but quit harassing Elizabeth."

His sister gave him a considering look and stalked away with an unladylike snort. The look on her face, however, had been remarkably satisfied and complacent.

Worth chuckled softly, leaving his hand where it was.

"Would you like me to pinch you again?" Elizabeth would dearly love to. Pinch him hard. How dare he act as if he really cared about her? Putting on a performance for his sisters was one thing, but he had no right to fool her. Not that Elizabeth had been fooled. She'd known all along he was putting on an act.

Worth raised an eyebrow a scant millimeter. "Don't tell me you didn't want me to get rid of him? The diameter of his biceps probably exceeds his IQ."

The arrogant, supercilious look on his face washed over her like a bucketful of cold water. He was so stupid he didn't even know what he'd done. Not that he'd done anything. She didn't want him to care for her. She certainly didn't care for him. She'd never care for someone so dumb. "A man with a minus IQ like you has no business throwing stones. He could be another Einstein for all you know."

"If he had a brain he wouldn't be on steroids."

For a second her voice failed her. Now he was acting as if he were jealous. No doubt that was for Cheyenne's sake, too. He'd made it all too clear what he'd meant by his comment about his sister playing into his hands. Now that Cheyenne was convinced, totally erroneously, that something existed between Worth and Elizabeth, she'd cease matchmaking.

Worth pretending to be jealous was absolute overkill. "You have no idea if he's on steroids," Elizabeth said. She knew darned well the issue wasn't steroids, but she wasn't about to explain to Worth she was furious because he'd tricked her. Not that he had. She'd known he was pretending. She didn't want him to be doing anything but pretending.

"With that muscle-bound body, he's sure to be. They all are."

"They all are? Better a muscle-bound body than a muscle-bound brain that can't think beyond stereotypes."

"This from the woman who talks about cowboys as if they were a lower form of life."

"If the shoe, excuse me, if the cowboy boot fits…" Suddenly remembering his hand still resting on her hip, Elizabeth, with exquisite self-control, removed it with the tips of her fingers in a blatant display of fastidious distaste.

The black look on Worth's face almost sent her racing for safety as he leaned down so his nose practically touched hers. "You might want to remember I know all your secrets, Red," he drawled, menace coating every word.

He didn't know all her secrets, and she couldn't believe after what he'd done, he dared to threaten her. "You are the lowest of the low, Worth Lassiter.. Pond scum has more redeeming qualities than you do." She refused to so much as blink. "I'd rather—" Swallowing the word *kiss* just in time, she dredged up other words, too angry to care if they made sense. "I'd rather touch what you shovel out of the barn than touch you."

He looked at her as if she'd lost her mind.

She didn't care what he thought. She didn't care about him. She refused to care. "You can go on television with my secrets and I don't care anymore. What do you think of that, Mr. Blackmailer?" Elizabeth snapped her fingers under his nose. "That's how much you scare me. What's more, I don't care if Cheyenne marries you off to ten women. I've had it with you and your blackmail. From now on, you hide behind somebody else. I don't want you to ever speak to me again." She was so angry with him, she shouted her last words.

It felt good to scream and shout. Liberating. She realized she'd wanted to shout at someone, anyone, from the moment she'd read Lawrence's letter.

Spinning around, Elizabeth took two quick steps and came to a dead halt. Every pair of eyes in the vicinity was locked on her and Worth. The shock on their faces made it clear they'd all heard her shouted words. It was less clear how they'd interpreted what they'd heard.

Knowing her face was crimson, Elizabeth took a deep breath, and looking straight at Cheyenne, met their speculation head-on. "Want to flip a coin to see who gets to push him in the stock tank?"

"I suppose you want an explanation for Elizabeth's temper tantrum last night," Worth said.

"Not particularly." Mary set a mug of coffee on the porch railing and sat in the chair next to Worth. "This visit's been good for Elizabeth. She was so pale and wan when she arrived. Lifeless. As if her spirit had died when her husband did."

Worth tried again. "Cheyenne's been matchmaking again."

His mother gave him a vague smile and looked down at the interminable lists which seemed a part of her hand these days. "You're such a challenge for her," she said absently.

He doggedly tried again. "I'm not interested in getting married now, and if I was, which, I repeat, I am not, Elizabeth is hardly the woman for me." He clamped his lips shut before he added a woman who was afraid of horses had no business on a ranch.

His mother made a tiny check on the paper. "You're the one who always claims Cheyenne usually knows what she's doing," Mary murmured without lifting her head.

"Not this time."

"I wonder... Was I supposed to check in with the hotel staff about the prenuptial dinner, or was Cheyenne doing that? Since Russ is hosting the dinner, maybe Elizabeth would want... I better phone Cheyenne." His mother picked up her mug and wandered back into the house.

Worth propped his feet on the porch railing and scowled at an early robin digging for worms under the cottonwood tree. Water droplets clung to flower stalks, the only visible sign of an early morning rain shower. The air smelled clean and refreshed.

Elizabeth always smelled clean and fresh. Like a baby after his bath.

He shook his head, trying to put one totally exasperating redhead out of his mind. Even though Russ had had red hair in his youth, he was calm, easygoing, slow to rile, a man who took his time making judgments and who believed in compromise. How he'd fathered a hot-tempered, know-it-all, uncompromising, stubborn redhead defied Worth's imagination.

He couldn't believe the way she'd erupted last night. After he'd gone to bed, he'd gone over in his mind again and again what had taken place, and for the life of him, he couldn't figure out what had set her off. She'd agreed to their little pretense.

He frowned at a sudden thought. Maybe Elizabeth had wanted those idiots nosing around her like she was a mare ready to mate. Worth made a disgusted sound as the truth hit him. He'd been trying to bolster her confidence and help her recover from her husband's death, and he'd obviously succeeded all too well. Elizabeth was apparently eager to remarry.

Which meant their little arrangement had become inconvenient for her. Too bad. She could look for a husband back in Nebraska.

The robin worked at pulling a fat worm from the ground. The worm kept coming and coming. It must go clear to China. China, now there was a subject a man could happily think about.

The Great Wall. Worth had seen pictures of the markets. Lots of red items. Silks, quilts, flags. Red.

He'd never been particularly attracted to red hair.

She'd love the Chinese babies. She loved all babies. All children. Even when she'd arrived, prickly and plastered with "Keep Away" signs, she'd responded lovingly to the children. Smiled at them. Warm, generous, accepting smiles.

Had she smiled at her husband like that? At the breakfast table? Over dinner? Before sex? After?

What difference did it make to him? The crazy redhead. Her husband must have been a saint. Imagine living with a volcano, never knowing when she was going to erupt. A man could get scorched. All that heat and passion focused on him.

He felt sorry for any man who was fool enough to fall in love with her. Just thinking about it made Worth glad he wasn't that man.

Disgusted with the way his body hardened at the thought of sharing a bed with a woman no man in his right mind would be attracted to, Worth slammed his feet to the floor and took off for his office.

Much of the day a nebulous anger which he refused to analyze simmered on the edges of his consciousness. It wasn't until he called the dealer's shop about the big hay baler he'd taken in two weeks ago for repairs and the shop foreman continued to give him the runaround that Worth found a worthy target for venting his spleen. Without raising his voice, he took the man apart, bone by bone.

Reducing the man to apologetic gibberish made Worth feel so much better, he went in search of Elizabeth.

He found her coming out of Jamie's room. She put a finger to her lips for silence. Silence suited Worth. "Put jeans on," he said quietly. "We're going riding."

"I'm not—"

His finger over her mouth hushed her. Her eyes shot darts at him. Worth grinned. "Be at the corral in five minutes."

He gave her fifteen minutes. If she wasn't there by then, he'd haul her out.

She showed up in seven. "I am not riding."

Looking at the jeans she wore, he said nothing as he handed over Rosie's reins.

Elizabeth accepted them without looking. "I can't keep going off leaving Jamie for your mother to take care of."

"We'll be back before he wakes up from his nap. I told Mom where we were going."

"I'm not riding today."

Worth wondered when she'd notice Rosie stood right behind her. Judging from the look in Rosie's eye, not long. Rosie thrust her long nose at Elizabeth, knocking her hat to the ground.

Elizabeth whirled around, her hand at her throat. "Oh. Rosie. You scared me half to death."

Rosie lowered her head, picked up the hat and presented it to Elizabeth. Elizabeth laughed as she accepted the hat. "Where did you learn to do that?" She scratched the mare's neck.

Worth swung up into his saddle. Hands resting on the saddle

horn, he gazed at the mountains. Not until he heard the creak of saddle leather behind him did he signal his horse to move.

Elizabeth had made up her mind to apologize to Worth. Not because she was wrong, and not because she cared what he thought of her, but because she did not want to be the cause of any unpleasantness in the midst of wedding festivities.

The only reason she'd agreed to ride was so she could apologize in private, but she had no intention of shouting her apologies to his back.

He sat tall in the saddle. As one with his horse. Elizabeth didn't think she'd ever seen a man so in tune with his surroundings, his life. She couldn't put her finger on it, but Worth seemed to flow through life instead of fighting it.

She eyed his broad shoulders. Hard work had put strong, solid muscles on his frame, yet his large, calloused hands could be gentle. With the foals. His nieces and nephew. With Jamie.

A jay called from a patch of scrub oak, his feathers bright blue against the new green leaves. The trail widened and Elizabeth urged Rosie to quicken her step until she walked even with Worth.

He slanted her an questioning look.

Elizabeth had to say something. "I noticed you at the computer all morning. Your mom said you sell horses over the Internet."

"I don't sell them over the Internet. I list what horses we have available. If a buyer is interested, he can e-mail or phone me. We try to put as much information on our site as we can, along with photographs of the horses, but buyers usually want to know something specific we haven't included. If my answers satisfy them, and they live a distance away, I'll send a videotape of the horse working. If they are still interested, I expect them to come to the Double Nickel and see the horse in person. We also advertise our stallions if someone has a mare he wants to breed. On another part of our site we sell cows and advertise our bulls."

"Sounds like a lot of work."

"Don't you mean you're surprised a cowboy is computer literate?"

He didn't make apologizing easy. "I'm sorry I got a little upset last night," she said, forcing out the words. "Our argument could have ruined Allie's party. I've already apologized to her and your mother."

"Apology accepted."

Where was the part where he returned her apology? She wouldn't have lost her temper last night if he hadn't pushed her too far. "After I thought about it," she said from between clenched teeth, "I realized you couldn't possibly have meant to act as selfishly as you did. It was very embarrassing having you paw me in front of a crowd of people which included my father."

Worth stopped his horse and pushed his hat to the back of his head. "When you think about it, I did you a favor."

"Did me a favor?" Hearing her voice rising, Elizabeth took a deep breath and forced herself to speak calmly. "You weren't doing me a favor. You were reinforcing Cheyenne's belief that we are interested in each other. Although how anyone in their right mind could possibly think..." There was no point in discussing that with him. "How you can call that doing me a favor, I can't imagine."

"Easy. It chased away the riffraff hanging around you. I assumed you weren't ready to replace your husband. I guess I should have asked if you wanted Cheyenne to fix you up with one of her friends."

"Yes, you should have." As if anyone could replace Lawrence.

It all came down to trust.

Loving again might not be so difficult. Trusting a man with her inner secrets was another matter altogether.

Elizabeth scowled at Worth. "Whether or not I'm looking for a husband is absolutely none of your business."

"Fine. You want my sister to set you up, so be it." He turned his horse. "Let's go back and I'll call her right now. Tell her we were just acting. Tell her you're free as a bird.

Which so-called gentleman do you prefer? Name him and I'll tell her to bring him right out.''

He was being deliberately obtuse. She wasn't looking for male companionship, and if he didn't know that, he should. ''I am not the least bit interested in any of them. That is so absolutely not the point. You didn't care what I wanted and you weren't doing me any favors. All you thought about was using me to outmaneuver your sister.''

Reining in his horse, he gave her an exaggerated look of surprise. ''I thought we had an agreement to help each other out until the wedding.''

''I didn't agree to pawing.''

Worth studied her face. ''Pawing? Or public pawing?''

She opened her mouth, then snapped it shut. Worth had kissed her more than once and she hadn't exactly objected.

Worth waited, an expression of polite interest on his face. No wonder he drove his sisters crazy.

Elizabeth was not his sister. ''I'm canceling our arrangement.'' Looking down at her hands clutching the saddle horn, she gave him the arguments she'd painstakingly worked out last night when sleep wouldn't come. ''We no longer need it. The prenuptial dinner is tomorrow night. The wedding the next afternoon. Cheyenne will be too preoccupied to worry about you until after the wedding. As for me, Russ has become so nervous about the wedding, he can barely remember his name, much less remember I'm around. He certainly won't be paying any attention to whether or not I'm riding horses.'' She took a quick peek at Worth.

His face gave no clue to his thoughts. Elizabeth resisted an overwhelming urge to fidget. ''I'm not going to let you blackmail me anymore. If you want to tell Russ I'm afraid of horses, go ahead.'' She stared straight ahead at Rosie's ragged ear. Rosie was a survivor. Elizabeth intended to be one, too. ''I can deal with the fallout.''

After a bit she heard Worth take a deep, slow breath. ''Yes, I know you can, but there won't be any fallout. I won't say anything to Russ.'' Leaning toward her, Worth adjusted her hat to better shade her face. "No more arrangement. Let's finish our ride."

She straightened her spine. "Yes, let's finish our ride."

Later, she couldn't have said where they rode. She had no memory of what they'd talked about. If they'd talked. What she'd seen.

She only remembered feeling better about herself. About life. Maybe the hope in Hope Valley was contagious. All she knew was that, overcoming one obstacle at a time, she was going to make it.

Worth sat in front of his computer, staring blankly at the dark screen. The sound of Elizabeth's voice drifted down from overhead. Jamie must have finished his nap.

The little boy had still been sleeping when they returned from their ride yesterday.

The decision whether to ask Elizabeth if she wanted to ride again today had been taken from his hands when prewedding jitters hit his mother with a vengeance midway through breakfast this morning. Elizabeth had become Mary's sounding board, her second-in-command, her anchor.

Russ had cravenly disappeared right after breakfast, mumbling about checking some cows. He hadn't been able to look Worth in the eye as he left.

Worth saw a side of Elizabeth he hadn't expected. Her crisis management skills, which would impress Thomas, clearly demonstrated why she'd thrived in the high-stress hotel business. He hadn't considered how much easier it is to handle someone else's crisis.

The faintest hint of baby powder scented the air. Jamie had spent the morning holed up in here with Worth while the madness flowed past the closed office door.

Worth liked having the kid around. He'd miss him when he left. His sisters had kids. He should spend more time with them. Their fathers would share.

Little boys needed a father. One of these days Elizabeth would have to find Jamie a father. Not one of those jerks

Cheyenne had dug up, but a man who'd love and appreciate her. She couldn't stay a widow forever.

Who'd take Jamie fishing?

He pictured Elizabeth squeamish at the thought of touching a worm and smiled. She'd do it for Jamie.

She was a good mother.

She'd make a good wife.

The man who married her would be a lucky man. Especially if she still had those green pajamas.

He didn't want to think about green pajamas. Or about the man who married her.

All this prenuptial bliss silliness softened a man's brain. Put thoughts there he didn't want to have. She was making him as crazy as she was. Two more days and she'd be gone.

He could kick back and relax. Enjoy his peace and quiet. No babies giggling. Or redheaded mothers laughing.

He looked forward to his solitude.

He could make travel plans. Reservations. He hadn't decided where he'd go first.

Marriage, a wife, a family, clipped a man's wings. Worth hadn't even spread his yet. He sure didn't want them clipped.

Abruptly yanking open a desk drawer, he pulled out some brochures. The island of Hawaii had ranches and volcanoes. There was a whaling village on Maui. Broad creamy beaches and swaying palm trees on all the islands. And everywhere couples strolling. Couples.

Not a single brochure showed a lonely male tourist.

CHAPTER EIGHT

WORTH handed Elizabeth a glass of wine after the wedding rehearsal. "Do you suppose Thomas bribed the weather gods so he could have the hotel gardens at their peak for Mom's outdoor wedding?"

"The columbines are gorgeous." Elizabeth had been afraid her outburst at Allie's party and her refusal to continue with his so-called arrangement would wreck any chance of a friendly relationship, but Worth behaved no differently toward her.

Elizabeth certainly didn't miss his kisses.

She sipped her wine and tried to think of something clever to say. "The rehearsal went well."

Worth raised a mocking brow. "It was a comedy of errors and you know it."

"Doesn't a bad dress rehearsal mean good luck for the opening night of a play? Maybe that applies to weddings, too."

"Lassiter women don't believe in normal weddings," he said dryly. "Maybe that's why they have successful marriages."

Elizabeth's fingers tightened around the stem of her glass. She didn't want to talk about successful marriages. "This is the first time I've seen The Green Room after dark. All these shades of green. It's lovely."

And lyrically romantic. Candles in pale pink glass globes flickered on every conceivable surface, while Tiffany-style lamps glowed like jewels. In the corner, a young man played soft, romantic mood music on a moss-green grand piano. Ordinarily the hotel's piano lounge, the room had been reserved for their private prenuptial dinner.

"Back when the St. Christopher Hotel was built in the late

131

1880s, ladies didn't go into the bar, and they didn't like to sit on display in the lobby, so this was the ladies' lounge.'' Worth eyed her over his wineglass. ''For someone run ragged today by my mother, you look very nice tonight.''

''I don't even want to know what nice means to a cattle-man.''

He laughed and took a drink of wine.

''You look good in a blue shirt,'' she blurted out. ''It matches your eyes.''

''Is that good like a steak is good?'' he asked gravely, his eyes warm with amusement.

She managed to laugh and hoped he didn't notice her body humming. Something it had a deplorable tendency to do more and more in his presence.

Blue eyes would haunt her dreams.

At dinner she sat between Zane Peters and Quint Damian. She enjoyed them both. Smart, humorous, good-looking men.

Neither would show up in her dreams.

Worth sat between two of his sisters, his head leaning toward Greeley as he focused on her conversation. They both grinned and Worth put his arm around his sister, whispering something in her ear which turned her grin into full-blown laughter.

''Amazing how young Mary looks when you consider she raised four of them. I can't imagine what it must have been like growing up in this family.''

Elizabeth turned to Quint Damian. ''Fun, I'd think.''

He smiled. ''Do I hear the voice of another only child?''

She nodded. ''I always envied my friends with brothers and sisters.'' Maybe it was the understanding on his face which led her to confess, ''I think that's why I wanted so badly to meet my stepbrother, but growing up, I never did. Then the hotel chain transferred me to Omaha, Nebraska, about an hour from Lincoln. I knew from my stepfather that his son taught in Lincoln. One day I took my courage in both hands and called him and invited him to meet me for dinner.''

"Greeley said you married him, so I'd guess the dinner was a success."

Elizabeth toyed with her fork. "I thought so."

He reached over and gave her elbow a sympathetic squeeze. "Mary can't say enough about how clever your son is. I think if Russ pulled out of the wedding now, Mary would insist she get to keep Jamie as her grandson."

Elizabeth took a gulp of wine to hide the wobbling of her lower lip. "Thank you," she managed to say.

Quint patted her arm and turned in response to a question from Cheyenne on his other side.

A lonely ache grew in her chest. The wine must be making her weepy. She couldn't cry. A prenuptial dinner was a happy occasion.

She assumed for everyone else it was.

Tomorrow night after the wedding, she and Jamie would spend the night at St. Chris's and fly out of Aspen the following morning.

Elizabeth felt confident that once they were married, Mary would drag Russ to visit his only daughter and grandchild. No doubt she and Jamie would come back to visit her father and Mary.

Those visits wouldn't be the same as this visit. They'd be less hectic. Less upsetting.

Less magical.

Why that should be so, Elizabeth didn't want to think about. She already knew the answer.

She forced down the dinner, drank her wine and smiled. And smiled and smiled. Smiled until the muscles of her face ached.

Every part of her ached.

Everyone toasted everyone else. The dinner went on forever. It was over much too soon.

The wedding. And then home.

To start her life over.

Elizabeth paced her bedroom floor, Jamie fussing unhappily in her arms. A new tooth had picked a poor time to come through, and Jamie had cried all the way back to the ranch.

In the hours since they'd returned from the prenuptial dinner, Elizabeth had rocked him endlessly as her normal remedies to ease his pain failed miserably. Jamie would doze for seconds, only to jerk awake and resume crying. She'd finally abandoned the rocker to walk the bedroom floor.

Her spirits had fallen so low, Elizabeth was in danger of tripping over them. She hadn't even been tempted to smile when she'd heard Mary sneak past the closed bedroom door on her way to what Mary mistakenly believed to be a *secret* rendezvous with Russ.

"How about another cold teething ring?" she asked Jamie, wiping his unhappy face with a tissue.

Worth opened his bedroom door as she stepped into the hallway. "Anything I can do?"

"I'm sorry. I didn't mean to wake you."

"I wasn't sleeping."

"I'm sorry," she said again, knowing he hadn't been able to sleep because of Jamie's crying. "I have another teething ring in the freezer. The cold numbs the gum, and this one has warmed up."

"Here." Worth held out his arms. "Give him to me."

When she came back up the stairs, Worth was walking up and down the hall, softly singing country music, rocking her son in his arms. Jamie, chewing on one of Worth's knuckles, rejected the plastic teething ring.

"I'll walk him awhile," Worth said.

The wide hallway ended at a window overlooking the ranch yard. Too exhausted to argue, Elizabeth sat on the low, upholstered bench under the window.

Shirtless, wearing a pair of unbelted blue jeans, Worth strolled up and down the hall on bare feet. Jamie fussed and chewed Worth's hand.

"He's going to bite through to the bone," Elizabeth said.

"He's just gumming me." Worth crooned a few more bars.

"Mom will make Russ happy," he said unexpectedly, walking away from Elizabeth.

"I hope Russ makes her happy."

At the end of the hall he turned and headed back in her direction. "Are you worried he won't? Is that why you looked so sad tonight?"

"No. I mean I wasn't sad. I'm not worried." The hall light was dim, but she sensed him studying her.

"It must be hard. I don't think any of us considered what an ordeal this would be for you."

"When will you believe I'm not against Russ getting re-married?" she asked in quiet exasperation.

"I didn't mean that." Worth made a U-turn and walked away. Jamie's fussing seemed to have somewhat lessened. "I meant any wedding must be difficult. Weddings can't help but bring back memories of your own wedding day." After a min-ute he added, "I'll bet neither your wedding nor your courtship were as crazy as what my sisters put us through." He pivoted and headed toward her, shaking his head, amusement threading his voice.

"No, they weren't crazy." Crazy had come later. After Jamie's birth. "Believe it or not, I used to be a calm, reason-able person, terrific in a crisis. In the hotel business, you have to be. My wedding ran like clockwork. Russ gave me away and my stepfather stood up with Lawrence. My maid of honor wore pale teal because it's her favorite color. I wanted every-one as happy as I was. I wore my mother's dress."

Elizabeth fell silent, remembering how beautiful she'd felt in the dress. Initially she'd hesitated to wear it, fearing it might be bad luck since her parents had divorced, but Lawrence had laughed at her superstitious fear.

For his own reasons.

Roses in shades of creamy white through delicate apricot had filled the church. The day had been warm even for eastern Nebraska, and the smell of roses had almost gagged Elizabeth when she'd walked into the church. By the time the ceremony ended, she'd grown accustomed to the strong odor.

A person could get used to anything.

Elizabeth thought about that, and thought about roses in June and realized what day it was. Midnight had come and gone. The sun would rise in a few hours. It was already the day of Russ's and Mary's wedding.

Words she hadn't intended saying came out in a rush. "Tomorrow would have been my third wedding anniversary."

Worth abruptly stopped, his back to her. After a minute he said, "Russ should have told us." Turning, he added quietly, "I'm sure Mom didn't know. She never would have scheduled her wedding the day before your anniversary."

Elizabeth shrugged. "Doesn't matter." It didn't. Little about her wedding or her marriage mattered now. Except Jamie. Jamie mattered.

"It does matter."

"Don't tell Mary. Don't mention it to anyone. I don't want Russ or Mary to feel bad. I could have said something when Russ first told me when they were getting married."

"Why didn't you?"

She shrugged again.

The silence lengthened. Only Worth's padding footsteps and Jamie's occasional teary hiccup broke it. Worth had walked the length of the hallway a dozen more times before he spoke. "You didn't mention it because you thought your father should have remembered your wedding day."

Elizabeth put her feet on the bench, wrapped her robe around her legs and hugged them to her chest. "Russ isn't good on dates."

"Russ can tell you the birthdate of every horse that foaled during his tenure on that Texas ranch," Worth said evenly.

"It's not easy raising a long-distance child," Elizabeth said. "I didn't help much. We moved to Europe when I was twelve. I convinced him to visit me there instead of me visiting him. Mom would sign the two of us up on tours. He'd come for a couple weeks, and touring filled the awkward places. After we returned from Europe, I went to camp or had a summer job, so I managed to avoid going to a ranch again. He spent more time with those horses than me. Why wouldn't he know more about them?''

After a few more turns, Worth said softly, ''I think Jimbo's finally worn himself out. I'll put him in bed.''

Elizabeth followed him, watching as he laid her son on his back and tucked a soft blanket over him. Leaning over, Worth gently kissed Jamie, then smoothed his hand over the sleeping baby's head. Jamie slumbered on.

Elizabeth leaned against the doorjamb. ''Thank you.''

Worth pulled her into the hallway and closed the door behind them. Facing her, he placed his hands lightly on her shoulders. ''You're scheduled to fly home the day after the wedding.'' He smoothed the side of her hair. ''I think you ought to stick around a few more days, Red.''

Her breath caught. He didn't want her to leave. A tiny tendril of pleasure started to unfurl before Elizabeth deciphered the emotion in his eyes. He felt sorry for her. ''Why should I stay?'' she asked coolly. ''Is it bad luck to fly on an anniversary no one's celebrating?''

''I don't think it's a good day for you to be alone.''

''Are you worried I'll go on a drinking binge? Overdose on sleeping pills? Maybe you think I'll light candles in front of a shrine to Lawrence's memory.'' She shrugged off his hands and fled to the end of the hall, to stand in front of the bench. Looking out the window, Elizabeth wrapped her arms around her chest.

''The stars are really twinkling tonight.''

She didn't turn around. ''They don't twinkle. Atmospheric dust makes them look like that. Solar pollution.''

''Another romantic illusion shattered,'' Worth said lightly.

Suddenly chilled, Elizabeth squeezed her arms. ''Sorry.'' The curt apology couldn't have sounded less sincere. She was past caring about romantic illusions. They were for children. And the blindly stupid. When you found out the truth, which you always did if it was an awful truth, it hurt a thousand times worse than if you'd known the truth from the beginning.

Worth rubbed her upper arms, bringing warmth. Because

rubbing made her blood flow, warmed the under layers of skin. No other reason. "It's late," she said sharply. "You'd better go to bed."

"You, too."

"I will."

"Tell me about your husband. Sometimes talking helps."

"Does it? Does talking mend a broken leg, cure cancer, heal a diseased body?"

His hands stopped moving and tightened on her upper arms. "It gives you an outlet for anger."

"My how-to-be-a-good-little-widow book talked about anger, too. How it is one of the first stages of grieving. Somewhere in there you finally come to acceptance. They make it sound like having a bad cold. You come down with it, are sick, then you're fine. They don't say how long recovery takes."

"I imagine it takes as long as a person needs."

"How I love answers that say absolutely nothing at all. Given by blathering idiots who know absolutely nothing, yet feel compelled to share their total lack of knowledge."

Worth gave a soft chuckle. "You can't get rid of me that easily."

"No? I had no trouble getting rid of Lawrence."

"He died. You're in no way responsible for his death."

Elizabeth was exhausted and emotionally drained. The only feeling she could whip up was anger at Worth for his mindless platitudes. What did he know? She felt like shocking him out of his complacent ignorance. "I'm not talking about his death. He left Jamie and me. Wrote me a nice...no, not nice at all... A long letter explaining why he was walking out on us, then walked. Just like that. We got home from the hospital; I fed Jamie and put him down to sleep. When I came out of the room we'd fixed up as a nursery, I found the letter taped to the kitchen table. I was reading it for about the eighth or ninth time when the policeman showed up. I started laughing when he told me Lawrence had been killed."

Worth's hands were dead weights on her arms. He said nothing. His silence didn't surprise her. The policeman had been so shocked, he'd wanted to call an ambulance and have her carted off to the hospital. Thoughts of Jamie had quickly brought Elizabeth to her senses.

Removing Worth's hands, she stared ahead at nothing. "I don't know why I told you. I burned the letter as soon as the policeman left, and I never told anyone about it. I would appreciate it if you forgot I said anything." She stepped around him and walked away.

Worth stood frozen at the end of the hallway, deeply disturbed as much by Elizabeth's empty voice as by what she'd said. He thought of his sisters coming to him when unhappiness and pain overwhelmed them, and he wondered how Elizabeth had endured. Who had she turned to? She said she'd told no one.

Her bedroom door closed quietly. So she wouldn't wake up her son. Did she ever think of her own needs?

One mystery had been solved. This was Elizabeth's secret. The one which had sent her into a panicky denial of having any secret when he'd asked about her fear of horses. He'd never have guessed this.

She wouldn't have let the secret slip if she hadn't been so weary, her spirits so depressed. He couldn't begin to imagine the thoughts going through her head as she witnessed everyone else's happiness during her visit.

He had no idea why her late husband had walked out on her. A coward who left a letter instead of facing the woman he'd married was beyond contempt.

Elizabeth blamed herself. She hadn't said so, but Worth never doubted for a second that she'd been second-guessing every word she'd ever said to her husband, every action she'd ever taken. The man didn't deserve a second thought.

No sound came from her bedroom. He pictured her lying in the dark crying.

His hand was on the doorknob before he knew what he was going to do. Enough light from the hall leaked into the room to show him the dark mound of her body. No sound of weeping came from her pillow. Her ragged breathing told him she was awake.

Worth walked quietly to the side of the bed. He could see her eyes, wide, owl eyes, staring up at him. Giant shudders racked her body. He brought a finger to his lips, then folded aside her covers and picked her up. She weighed nothing. Other than one quick gasp when he bent over the bed, she made no sound.

In his room, he laid her on his unmade bed and pulled the covers over her. Without removing his jeans, he crawled in beside her and drew her into his arms, holding her tight against him. He felt the chill of her body through her thin pajamas, and methodically he massaged her, much as he rubbed a newborn colt. Gradually her shudders slowed, finally stopping, and her breathing leveled out.

"My stepfather talked a lot about his son," Elizabeth said, as if there had been no break in their conversation. "I could hardly wait to meet him. When I was little, I used to pretend he was my real brother instead of a stepbrother. Later, I was glad he wasn't my real brother. Because then I could fall in love with him."

Worth altered the rhythm of his strokes, slowing, gentling. As he'd comforted Jamie earlier. "You didn't meet as children?"

Her head shook against his chest, her hair tickling his skin. "He didn't come to Mother's wedding. His mother called and said he was sick. We all felt bad. Mother sent him a piece of wedding cake. I know now he didn't want to come. His mother didn't want him to come either, so she lied for him. Apparently she believed my stepfather would one day come to his senses and come begging back to her. She was a sick, bitter woman."

Who'd infected her son, Worth guessed. "Didn't he ever visit his father?"

"Children of divorced parents travel a lot between parents. When I got shipped out to stay with Russ, Lawrence got shipped in to stay with his father. Once we moved to Europe, Lawrence stopped coming. Camp, jobs. Like me, so I didn't think anything of it. My stepfather would fly back to the States and visit Lawrence.''

She fell silent, and Worth patiently waited.

"I thought I knew everything there was to know about Lawrence. My stepfather spoke proudly and often of Lawrence's grades, his accomplishments, articles published in school journals. He was editor of his college yearbook. My stepfather took pictures whenever he saw Lawrence, so I knew what he looked like.''

Her hands moved restlessly. Worth captured one and massaged her fingers. Her wrist felt thin and fragile.

"Lawrence looked like a younger version of my stepfather. He had the same voice, some of the same mannerisms. I love my stepfather, so it was easy for me to fall in love with Lawrence. My mother is so happy with John. I expected to be happy with Lawrence. I felt as if I knew him.''

She spoke in a vague, disconnected voice, as if reciting something by rote. "I didn't know how much he resented his father divorcing his mother, how much he resented my mother. Mother didn't even meet my stepfather until three years after his divorce.''

Worth smoothed down her hair, reluctant to interrupt her flow of words.

"My stepfather's in the military, and we normally lived in housing on the base, adequate, but not always spacious. When Lawrence came to visit, he usually had to stay in my room, a room my mother designed for a little girl, a room filled with little girlish things Lawrence was told not to touch. Lawrence believed his father preferred me to his own son.''

Suspecting where her story was headed, Worth clamped his jaws shut, holding in words and emotions which if loosed might frighten her back into her self-imposed silence.

"In the letter he told me he hated me. Said he'd hated me from the time he was ten. He married me and coldly, deliberately impregnated me. Those are the words he used to describe his son's conception. 'Coldly and deliberately impregnated' me. The act had nothing to do with love. Not even with lust. Only with revenge.''

She made an odd sound. "It's funny when you think about it. You thought I came to Colorado for revenge, when I'm the last person who'd do anything for revenge. Not now. Not after what Lawrence's sick and twisted thinking led him to do. I thought Jamie was our hope for the future. I was so happy, but I was wrong. Jamie was Lawrence's revenge on the past. From the beginning he intended to leave me as soon as I had 'the child.''

Worth was glad her husband was beyond earthly retribution. He'd never believed physical violence solved anything, but coldheartedly beating Lawrence to a pulp might have proved a temptation impossible to overcome.

"Lawrence rejoiced that Jamie was male. He said my stepfather and I would find out what Lawrence's life had been like, growing up without a father. His mother died of cancer while he was in college. He blamed that on us, too. Said he wanted me to know how his mother had suffered, raising a son by herself.''

Amazement colored her words as she added, "He actually believed raising Jamie would be a punishment to me." She paused. "He never held Jamie. I thought he was nervous. Some men are nervous with newborns." She fell silent again.

Worth had no words to console her. A dictionary full of words wouldn't have helped him. Her husband's cruelty could not be erased with sympathy or indignation.

The utter stupidity and waste were beyond Worth's comprehension. How could Elizabeth possibly have fallen in love with the kind of man who would desecrate that love?

She turned into him, wrapping an arm around his waist. Her breath warmed his skin. Her heart beat against his bare chest. He listened to her breathing and smelled baby powder mingling with the perfume she'd worn to dinner.

He hadn't realized it was possible to despise anyone as much as he despised her dead husband.

"I told everyone Lawrence was going to the grocery store

to pick up something for dinner. He was killed only a few blocks from our house," she said dully. "I never told my stepfather about the letter. If he ever found out, he would be devastated and blame himself." After a long pause, she added, "Mother could never keep it secret from him." She spoke again after an even longer pause. "And Russ would tell Mother."

The haunting, eerie howl of a distant coyote came through the open window. Another coyote answered the first. Male coyotes bonded with their mates and helped with their young. Calling a man like Lawrence Randall a low-down, dirty coyote insulted coyotes.

Elizabeth stiffened against him and made a funny little sound. "I can't believe I told you my pathetic tale. You must think I'm pitiful."

The humiliation and self-loathing in her voice angered him. He couldn't imagine how she'd borne her solitary burden for so long. "I'm glad you told me."

"It's too easy to talk in the dark. Late at night, tired, a person lets her defenses down. I must have had too much wine with dinner. You listen too well. It's seductive." She hesitated. "I hope you'll forget all this."

"Already forgotten," Worth lied.

Horses neighed in the pasture. They'd scented the coyotes.

"I should go back to my bed and let you sleep."

"If you want to. Or you can stay here for a while longer."

"I haven't been held for so long."

Rage swept through him at the mixture of apology and shame in her voice. When he'd brought his emotions under firm control, he said, "I like holding you. You smell like Jimbo."

"It makes a person question everything. Finding out how wrong I was. I truly believed he loved me and wanted his child. I've asked myself over and over again how he could have fooled me so completely. How I could have been so blind and stupid. How he could have done it. I could almost understand if there was another woman. But to plan so coldly to have a son in order to abandon him. I'll never understand that.''

Worth thought it defied understanding.

''I should feel sorry for him, that his hate outweighed what Jamie and I could give him. I think how joyless and barren his life was. He was brilliant, you know. He could have had so much.''

She was silent so long Worth thought she'd fallen asleep.

''Mostly I'm angry at him,'' she said. ''For hurting Jamie. For deceiving me. Do you want to know something really sick? I think I'm mostly angry because he humiliated me.''

The self-condemnation in her voice ripped at Worth's guts. She had nothing to condemn herself for. Nothing. ''He didn't humiliate you,'' he said evenly. ''There's nothing wrong with loving.''

''How could I love him? Maybe I didn't. I wonder now, but maybe that's only because of what he did to me. I don't know. Maybe I just wanted what my mother has. She's so happy with my stepfather.'' She paused. ''I thought Lawrence loved me. I thought he loved his son. I trusted him and he betrayed me. He was right about one thing. Sometimes I think I can't bear it that Jamie will grow up without a father. A boy needs a father.''

The last words were mere whispers against his chest as exhaustion won out and sleep claimed her. Unwilling to disturb her, Worth waited a long time before gingerly sliding a numb arm from beneath her head. With his other arm, he tucked her securely against him.

He'd heard people say their hearts ached for someone and assumed the words were merely a figure of speech. Not until now did he understand the crushing physical pain in one's chest at witnessing another's suffering. He wished she'd cried. Perhaps her pain had passed beyond the solace of tears.

Because she blamed herself for her husband's contemptible behavior, maybe she punished herself by refusing to give in to the weakness of tears. No wonder she was too thin, too brittle.

Worth wanted to shoulder her pain, alleviate her suffering. He was big and strong.

He'd never felt so helpless.

Elizabeth slept soundly, her body a featherweight warmth curled into him, her arm wrapped around his middle.

His body stirred and tightened. He wanted her.

At that moment he hated himself almost as much as he hated her dead husband. She didn't need another man using her to satisfy his base needs. She needed a friend. A brother.

His body refused to listen.

Setting his jaw, Worth folded one hand under his head and clenched the other at his side. Deliberately he forced himself to mentally compose a list of chores which needed to be done after the wedding.

From a distant hillside coyotes mocked his efforts.

As if they somehow knew about his body's heavy arousal.

Worth doggedly continued with his list of chores. He fell asleep somewhere between mowing the alfalfa and inspecting the irrigation ditches.

Toes sliding up and down his lower leg woke him. Worth didn't move, didn't open his eyes. A hand delicately explored his bare chest.

"I know you're awake. Your breathing changed." Inches from him, Elizabeth's voice came softly out of the darkness.

He opened his eyes, but couldn't see her face. His skin burned where she touched it. He sucked in air as she found one of his nipples. And wondered what she intended. Wondered if she could feel what her touch was doing to him. He cleared his throat. "Grandpa Yancy let me in on a secret when I was about ten."

Her hand moved across his chest. "It's a night for secrets."

The sultry tone in her voice would have been more convincing without the underlying uncertainty. Seducing a man appeared to be a new experience for her. If that was what she was doing. "The trick with women is to remember how it is with horses."

She went still, her hand and toes not moving, while she puzzled out his words. "What does that mean?" she finally asked.

Worth carefully refrained from touching her. "When a stallion approaches a mare, he does it cautiously. A lot of people think the stallion runs things, but the mare is the one who decides when and if she's ready to mate. A stallion who ignores her signals to keep away risks a chestful of flying hooves."

More time elapsed. "What if the stallion's not interested?"

He smiled in the dark. "Trust me, he's interested."

Her fingers slowly came to life, tiptoeing down his chest. "He doesn't find the mare embarrassingly aggressive?"

Worth found himself embarrassingly unprepared, but he feared she'd read rejection into his saying so. "As much as he likes green pajamas," Worth found the buttons and toyed with them, "the only thing he finds her is overly dressed."

"Oh."

Before she could close her mouth, he joined their lips, kissing her slowly, deeply, thoroughly. She lay perfectly still as if focusing all her attention on what he was doing to her mouth. And what she almost shyly began doing to his.

Outside false dawn lighted the sky. Birds twittered awake. No one else would be stirring for a while.

Worth could take his time. Give her what pleasure he could. Leisurely he slipped one button after another through the buttonholes. Her breath caught about the third button, and he lifted his head, pausing until she made a tiny, impatient move. Nibbling her bottom lip, he undid the last two buttons.

Her breathing grew more ragged with each button, and she clutched his shoulders as he opened her pajama top. Not to push him away.

Two could play the nipple game. He'd been right. Her breasts were exactly the right size. Her skin was softer, warmer than he'd imagined. Her chest rose and fell and she moved restlessly against his hands. He lowered his mouth, finding the tip which had tantalized him those million years ago in the kitchen. Her fingernails dug tiny trenches in the flesh of his shoulders.

He thought she probably didn't even notice when he removed her pajama bottoms. Her belly was soft, her legs warm and sleek. He slipped his hand between her thighs to a juncture of incredible heat. The explosion which followed didn't surprise him at all.

Elizabeth lay bonelessly on the bed and marveled that a year of marriage had not taught her this. After Lawrence had left, she'd missed the closeness, missed having a solid bulk at her back, the warmth and smell of a man in her bed. A soft giggle slipped out.

"What's so funny?"

She couldn't tell him.

Why couldn't she? She'd trusted him enough to be lying beside him stark naked. Not that the little joke was easy to put into words, especially when she didn't want to discuss Lawrence while in bed with Worth. "If I'd known about that," she said carefully, "I might have ignored my widow book and looked for comfort before."

An incredulous silence met her remark, then Worth started to laugh, choking it off immediately, as if he'd remembered the sleeping baby down the hall.

She remembered something else and reached for the waistband of his jeans. "Isn't the stallion supposed to take off his clothes, too?"

He grabbed her hand. "A stallion mates to breed the mare. I'm afraid you caught me unprepared."

Elizabeth froze as the meaning of his words sank in. "When did you remember that? Just now or before you..." She couldn't finish the question.

He didn't answer immediately. "Does it matter?"

His response told Elizabeth everything she needed to know. She snatched her hand away, her knuckles burning where they'd touched his jeans. The fact that his jeans bulged in front did nothing to lessen her humiliation. Her pajamas had disappeared, and she pulled the covers up to her neck. "You know it matters or you would have answered the question," she said bitterly. "I thought we were making love, but you were making pity."

"I wasn't—"

"Did you feel sorry for the poor, abandoned widow, or were you afraid I'd pitch a fit if you rejected me?"

"I wanted to do it for you, Elizabeth. Can't you accept the gift?"

"How many women have you given that *gift* to?" She put all the sarcasm she could muster into the word gift. He couldn't answer the question, not in any way which would appease her, so she didn't bother waiting for him to think up a lie. "I'm a charity case, like Rosie, aren't I? The mare nobody wanted because she was bony and ugly and half-dead. Where are my pajamas?"

He handed them to her. "There's a small drugstore not far from St. Chris's. I can sneak away during the wedding reception and buy—"

"Brains? I doubt they sell them," Elizabeth snapped, yanking up her pajama bottoms under the covers. She thrust her arms into the top. "Don't buy anything on my account."

"Maybe it would be on my account."

"Oh sure. And maybe aliens from outer space are going to sing at the wedding today." The buttons on her top fought her clumsy fingers. "You know what your trouble is, Worth Lassiter? You're dishonest. You never tell anyone when you don't want to do something. You smile, and you do it, even when a person doesn't want you to do it, and then you whine about all you have to do for everyone else. Did you ever stop to think maybe a person would rather have honesty than char—"

She clamped her mouth shut at the sound of footsteps in the hall. A quick look at Worth's window disclosed a fuchsia glow above the horizon. Elizabeth's hands froze on the last button as a knock sounded at the door.

Worth heard his mother call his name. Having little choice, he answered.

With a tiny squeak Elizabeth scooted down in the bed and flipped the covers over her head.

Mary opened the door and stuck her head inside.

"Would you do me a favor? Jamie wants breakfast, and I can't find Elizabeth. She must have gone for a walk."

"Sure, I'll go get him right now."

"Here he is." Mary opened the door and came in, Jamie in her arms. "I have a million things to do before the wedding today or I'd feed him," Mary said apologetically. "I'm sure Elizabeth will return soon."

Worth could feel Elizabeth practically quivering at his side. He didn't dare look in her direction.

Mary started toward the bed with Jamie. Worth leaped from under the covers. "Here. I'll take him."

"Why in the world are you sleeping with your jeans..." Her voice faltered and died as she looked beyond Worth.

Impossible not to turn around and see what had drawn her attention. A nicely-rounded bottom covered in green lay frozen in the center of his bed. In his haste to get out of bed before his mother neared it, he'd tossed the covers too far.

His mother thrust Jamie in Worth's general direction and said loudly, "Here he is. I'm going now. I'll be in my room if you need me. Just knock on my closed door."

Taking Jamie, Worth couldn't decide whether to hug his mother or laugh in her face. He opened his mouth to explain.

"Morning." Russ's voice boomed from the hallway. "Where is everyone?"

Mary jumped, her uneasy gaze shooting to Worth before she scooted toward the bedroom door. "Go away. It's bad luck for the groom to see the bride before the wedding on their wedding day."

Worth leaned down and flipped the covers over Elizabeth's backside.

"Seeing you could never be bad luck." Russ beat Mary to

the open bedroom door. "There's Jamie. Where's Elizabeth? I wanted to eat breakfast with my daughter and my grandson."

"I thought maybe…she likes to walk…" Mary tried to shoo Russ out of the bedroom. "I have a million things to do, and I'm sure you do, too. Worth is going to feed Jamie."

Jamie was hanging over Worth's arm, jabbering at the bed. Worth hoped the sounds the little boy was making didn't sound as much like "Ma Ma Ma" to Russ as they did to Worth.

"I guess I can feed my grandson." Russ extended his arms, then froze. "Elizabeth?"

CHAPTER NINE

Worth swung around. A tendril of red hair peeked from beneath the covers, standing out against the white pillowcase like a red flag waving in front of a bull.

"What are you doing in Worth's bed?" Angry disbelief coated Russ's every word.

Jamie screwed up his face and started to cry.

"Now, Russ, don't jump to any wrong conclusions," Mary said in a soothing voice, patting his arm, "I'm sure there's a logical explanation."

He pushed away her hand. "What explanation can there be for my daughter sleeping with your son except the obvious one?"

Bouncing Jamie in his arms, Worth looked from Russ's angry face to his mother's apprehensive one. A chilling sense of the inevitable hung over him like an executioner's sword.

"Come out of there before you suffocate," Russ harshly ordered.

Elizabeth slowly emerged from the covers. Red hair spilled over her shoulders with wild abandon, highlighting flushed cheeks and guilt-filled eyes. She was the picture of a woman who'd been caught in the wrong man's bed the morning after a night of making mad, passionate love.

Every muscle in Worth's body tightened, then anger flared at her ability to arouse him even in the most embarrassing and incriminating of circumstances. If she was going to run around in those green pajamas, she ought to fix them so they stayed buttoned, he thought savagely. Catching the direction of his gaze, Elizabeth looked down and immediately clutched the edges of her pajama top together. If Russ had missed their unbuttoned state before, no way he could have missed her convulsive movement.

Jamie had recovered from his fright and chattered happily to his mother as he drooled down Worth's shoulder. Worth wiped the baby's chin. Jamie responded with a toothy grin.

No one else grinned. They were frozen in a tableau of shock.

Worth wanted to shout at Russ. He wanted to walk away.

Elizabeth couldn't have made it clearer she wanted no more favors from him. Let her sort out the mess. Let her placate her father. Explain. If it could be explained.

Worth wanted to point out Russ and Mary had been sleeping together, but he knew Russ would reject the comparison. Russ and Mary had committed to each other. Their wedding today was merely public acknowledgment of that commitment.

Russ was old-fashioned enough to expect the same kind of commitment from a man who slept with his daughter. Worth couldn't think of any explanation or argument which would change Russ's mind.

He could hardly say Elizabeth had seduced him. That all he'd been doing was comforting her.

His mother had fixed her gaze on the huge silver belt buckle attached to the belt hanging from the corner of Worth's dresser mirror. Beau had won the buckle in Ft. Worth, Texas shortly after Beau and Mary got married. Worth had been conceived that night.

Mary Lassiter had raised her children to do the right thing. She wouldn't say a word to Worth no matter what he did, but he knew how she'd feel about her son acting less than honorably.

His mother loved her prospective husband and she loved her son. Starting her marriage with enmity between the two men would cause her enormous pain. Worth couldn't put his mother through that.

He didn't have to like the only choice available to him. Without a doubt this was his punishment for celebrating shedding his responsibilities. His penalty for thinking life owed him because he'd done his duty without complaint. Despite

Elizabeth's accusation to the contrary, he hadn't complained. He should have known she'd never understand.

She sat still and silent, her wide, staring eyes the only color in a white face. Worth gave her a tight-lipped smile. "I suppose we should have mentioned our plans earlier. Elizabeth didn't want to steal the limelight from you at your wedding."

"Mentioned what?" Russ demanded.

Images rolled across Worth's brain. China's Great Wall. Florida beaches. Hawaiian palm trees. London. Paris. Freedom. Adventure. He deliberately blanked his mind and said firmly, "Elizabeth has agreed to marry me."

Elizabeth opened and shut her mouth like a trout. Only an idiot or a blind man would believe she'd heard about his marriage proposal before this very second.

An idiot or a father.

Russ grabbed Worth's free hand, shaking it so violently, it was a wonder Worth's arm didn't detach at the elbow. "Congratulations. I couldn't be more thrilled."

Mary looked every bit as stunned as Elizabeth.

Worth tried to tell himself it wouldn't be too bad. He'd always planned to marry. Have children. One day. So what if one day was supposed to be far in the future? He and Elizabeth ought to be able to muddle through. It wasn't as if he had in mind anyone else to marry. He liked Jamie.

He'd bury his frustration in Elizabeth's body.

"Another Lassiter wedding," Mary said with forced gaiety. "Won't everyone be surprised when I tell them at the wedding today? Speaking of weddings, time marches on even when there's suddenly another engagement. I don't know about the rest of you, but I have a ton of things to do." She bounced a troubled look off Worth.

He gave her a reassuring smile. He wouldn't let her down. "I imagine we all have plenty to do." Jamie gnawed on his shoulder. "And the first order of business is to feed Jimbo."

Then he'd throw away all the travel brochures he'd collected over the years.

"No. I don't want to announce at your wedding today that Worth and I are planning to get married."

Overwhelming relief swept over him. Elizabeth didn't want to marry him. He wasn't about to force her.

If a little niggle of regret sneaked in, Worth blamed it on the green pajamas.

"Why not?" Russ asked fiercely, his face dark with anger.

Worth watched Elizabeth's pale pink lips move. Heard the words coming from her mouth. And belatedly saw her entire grand plan as clearly as if she'd drawn him a picture.

She was the greatest actress it had ever been his misfortune to meet.

"I'm afraid I'm going to be selfish," she said, a coy, self-conscious smile on her face. "Please don't tell anyone today about Worth and I getting married. I want my own moment of glory, not to share your wedding day. We can have a party after you return from your honeymoon, Russ, and you can make a formal announcement of Worth's and my engagement then."

Worth smiled and chatted and forced down the food the servers put in front of him. He accepted congratulations on his mother's marriage and toasted her and Russ. He returned his sisters' hugs and danced the first dance with his niece Hannah.

All the while seething with impotent fury.

He should have paid more attention when Elizabeth said she hated having her son grow up without a father. Should have realized she'd selected a replacement father for Jamie.

Just thinking of her simpering smirk when she begged Russ to wait before announcing their engagement made him want to toss her in the champagne fountain.

What a sucker he'd been last night. Swallowing hook, line and sinker her preposterous tale of woe. It was a wonder she hadn't choked on laughter.

Or her lies.

His fingers curled into fists as he remembered the way he'd

lapped up the undoubtedly fictitious details of her husband's farewell letter. The pity he'd felt. The anger at her husband.

Lawrence Randall had been lucky to escape her.

No wonder she'd been so angry this morning when he'd behaved responsibly. An unplanned pregnancy would have made his marrying her a sure bet. Only a man blinded by lust—and ego—would believe a woman had suddenly developed a craving for his body. A decidedly tardy realization came to him. Elizabeth had responded when he kissed her, but not once had she initiated a kiss.

Until this morning. As part of her trap.

He was getting exactly what he deserved.

The rest of his life. Tied to a treacherous, lying redhead.

After the ceremony, everyone said it had been the most beautiful Lassiter wedding ever. Elizabeth would have to take their word for it. Not only because she hadn't attended any of the other Lassiter weddings, but because she had little memory of this one.

There had been no ritual giving away of the bride to the groom. No bridesmaids or flower girls. Mary's daughters, son, sons-in-law and grandchildren had gathered with her. Elizabeth and Jamie had stood with Russ. All joined in joyous approval and celebration of the marriage. It had been Cheyenne's idea. A symbol of love and support for the bridal couple.

Elizabeth had tried to feel joyous. Tried to focus on Mary and Russ exchanging vows, but anger and humiliation held her in their grip. This morning she'd thought she and Worth were making love, and the experience had been achingly beautiful for her. Until Worth had tarnished everything by making it clear what had happened wasn't an act of love; it was an act of philanthropy. He'd been taking care of the wounded. The unwanted.

She would have preferred selfish, sterile sex for its own sake. His pity enraged her. How dare he feel sorry for her?

An inconvenient honesty made her admit she was partially to blame. Letting everything pour out about Lawrence.

She hadn't walked to Worth's room.

Okay, she'd touched him first, but she hadn't held a gun to his head.

His announcement that they were getting married had stunned her. Until she'd realized why he'd said it. Vintage Worth Lassiter. Accepting responsibility. Being a martyr to the end. Only one circumstance had stopped her from jumping out of his bed and dramatically proclaiming to the world she'd rather walk bare naked through downtown Aspen than marry Worth Lassiter. She couldn't spoil Russ and Mary's wedding day.

When Mary and Russ returned from their honeymoon, she would tell her father she was not marrying Worth.

Worth no more wanted to marry her than she wanted to... That was the most humiliating realization of all. For the teeniest part of an instant, following Worth's announcement...

She'd wanted it to be true.

Laughter drew Elizabeth's eyes across the room to where Greeley twirled a giggling Jamie around the dance floor. Nearby Quint danced solemnly with Hannah while Allie attempted to teach Davy a complicated dance step. Playpens had been set up along one wall, and Cheyenne's nanny watched over Harmony and Virginia, the latter playing with her toes while her younger cousin slept.

Elsewhere Thomas twirled Mary to the sounds of a small string ensemble, and Zane danced with Cheyenne.

Elizabeth looked down at her glass of wedding punch. She refused to scan the ballroom to see who Worth danced with.

The hair on the back of her neck tingled, and she turned so quickly she almost poured red punch on his elegant gray suit.

Worth pried her fingers off the glass and set it on a nearby table. "I believe this is our dance." He swung her onto the floor, critically eying her hair which she'd pinned to the back of her head in a sophisticated sweep. "Don't plan on wearing your hair pinned up once we're married."

"Be quiet. Someone will hear you." So far she'd managed to keep any news of their mythical engagement from spreading.

"I suppose you want a fancy wedding and party like this. Will Russ pay for it, or am I to be stuck with that, too?"

She didn't appreciate his treating the matter as a joke. "I'm not marrying you, and you know it."

"I didn't hear you arguing the point earlier this morning."

She stared at him in disbelief. "Excuse me? I am not the one who made the grand announcement. The only reason..." Her voice dried up as the anger in his eyes hit her in the face like a fiery furnace blast.

"I led myself right down the garden path, didn't I? You flaunted your body in those sexy green pajamas, and my brain rolled over and died." He spoke in an easygoing drawl, a fixed smile on his face. "I have just one question, Red. Did you plan the whole thing or just get lucky?"

Each coldly-drawled, nightmarish word pummeled her in the midsection. The blood drained from her head. She had to get away from him. He tightened his grip.

"Smile, Red." His own smile held all the friendly warmth of a coiled rattlesnake. "A wedding reception is supposed to be a happy occasion." If possible, his smile grew even grimmer. "I find it difficult to believe Russ was in on your plan."

His insinuations numbed her brain, and she struggled to make sense of his anger. "Are you accusing me of setting things up so you'd be forced to ask me to marry you?"

"I'm sorry I didn't put up much of a battle. It must have been boringly easy for you. You're good, Red, real good. Your failure to cry should have clued me in, but I'm such a sap, I convinced myself your pain was too deep for tears."

She'd gone from being pitiful to being despicable. It was hilariously funny. One day she'd see the humor in it and laugh herself silly. One day. Not now. She was too furious.

She definitely was not hurt. Worth Lassiter didn't have the power to hurt her. Burying the pain, she gave him an admirably cool smile. "You certainly are a sap. I've been patting myself on the back all morning at how well my plan worked out. The toughest part was getting Jamie to fuss and keep you awake.

I certainly couldn't count on happenstance, could I? I stuck a pin in his diaper. Worked pretty good, didn't it?''

He gave her a narrow-eyed look. ''You wouldn't hurt Jimbo.''

''I certainly would. Of course Russ was in on it. We planned the whole thing on the phone before I came. You didn't notice I was wearing a watch last night. Your bad luck, because it was actually a beeper. So I could signal Russ at just the right time. Clever, right? And by the way, thanks for all your help. I was about to give up on you. I thought I was actually going to have to go to your room and tell you I was cold and ask if I could climb in bed with you. Lucky for me you're such a do-gooder, isn't it? Russ thought he'd have to threaten the old shotgun to force you into marrying me, but no, Mr. Sees His Duty and Does It leaped right in. I'll bet you're sorry now you left those jeans on.''

''I was sorry then.''

''Too bad.'' A deep breath gave her a second head of steam, and she plunged ahead. ''Russ didn't even get a chance to go into his full-blown, outraged-daddy routine. He'll pout about that for a long time, but I guess we can't have everything, can we? After all, we got the main prize. You. The man I'm dying to marry because, not only is he Mother Nature's gift to women, he's such a dope if we ever had any children they'd have the IQ of an earthworm, and of course, it's always been my secret dream to live on a ranch because if there is one thing I'm absolutely crazy about, it's horses.'' She had to stop, not because she'd run out of words, but because Worth clamped his hand over her mouth.

''You have to admit, you leaped on my proposal.''

She bit his fingers, hard, and he snatched them away. ''I didn't leap on any proposal because there wasn't any. You didn't ask me anything. Oh no, Mr. Sacrifice Everything For His Family stood there in the middle of his bedroom where he had dragged me and announced to the entire world I was marrying him, never mind whether I wanted to marry him, because he knew I would because of course he not only knows my mind he knows he's so wonderful that a broken-down, rejected widow would leap on the chance to live on a ranch because she's so crazy—''

He kissed her. Not a soft, seductive kiss, but a hard, shut-your-mouth kiss.

Elizabeth refused to close her eyes. She scowled at his eyebrow and tried not to feel the warmth of his lips. He had a nice eyebrow. Not black and beetling. It fit his face. Not that his eyebrow interested her anymore than the rest of him. He'd kissed her long enough. Bringing her hands to his face, she pushed his head back.

They stood in a hallway. So busy telling him off, she'd missed that he'd waltzed her out of the ballroom. Muted strains of music came through the open doorway. The music did nothing to charm her savage breast. "Aren't you afraid someone will see us and get the wrong idea? They might think we're sneaking up to one of the rooms. This time I'd make sure you took off your clothes. I wouldn't want you wiggling out of marriage through a technicality. I'm not wearing a watch today, but one of my earrings is a beeper. To make sure we're caught with both of us stark naked in bed. Just another example of my devious plan to snare you for my husband.''

"Maybe I was wrong," he said mildly, backing her up against the nearest wall.

"Worth Lassiter, wrong? I don't think so. The world would come to an end at such a revolutionary idea. No, no, no, Worth Lassiter could never be wrong.''

"I didn't force you to agree to marry me. Even you have to admit the situation looked bad.''

"It doesn't look bad to me. I got what I wanted. You. Am I ever excited. I can hardly wait to call up my mother and tell her I'm getting married again, which is something I've been desperate to do ever since my last husband ripped out my heart—oops, that's right, he didn't. You know how it is, you work so hard to take on a role, sometimes you forget to let it go. Naturally, he's not even dead. He's just pretending so he can get his cut of all your money. And don't forget the ranch. We really want part of your ranch.''

Elizabeth flattened her palms against the wall behind her. To support her. "And Jamie, he's been great, hasn't he? I'll bet you thought he was a baby. Actually, he's a midget. My lover, in fact. I have tons of lovers. Too bad you didn't know that before you made your excruciatingly funny noble gesture. If I had any integrity whatsoever, I'd free you from your obligation, but I could have done that this morning, couldn't I? And since I didn't, well, if I were you, I wouldn't count on me doing it now.''

"You're not planning to marry me.''

"You haven't been listening. Marrying you is my life's ambition.''

"It would have been interesting.'' He braced himself with a hand on the wall near her head. The anger had faded from his eyes. An amused smile played over his mouth.

Elizabeth failed to find any amusement whatsoever in the situation. Rubbing her palms up and down the wall, she felt every nub and weave in the textured wallpaper. "Would have? Be careful or I'll have to sue you for breach of promise. There were two witnesses to your grand announcement.''

"Three.'' He grinned. "You forgot Jimbo.''

She ignored that. "You don't think Russ is going to let a prize like you get away, do you?''

"I know Russ will be disappointed. He wants you near.''

Elizabeth stared past Worth's shoulder. On the opposite wall painted stylized lilies in shades of rose and green stretched elegantly from the ceiling. She couldn't believe how easily her father had accepted Worth's lie. As for Mary... "Your mother won't be disappointed. She thinks like you do. That I trapped her precious son into marriage.''

"Elizabeth, I believe I owe you an apology. I should have known you were as much a victim of unfortunate circumstances as I was. I saw myself chain...that is, I panicked. I'm sorry.''

The man had no end of ways to hurt her. "Think nothing

of it. I'm used to men thinking being married to me is a fate worse than death.'' Her attempt at a laugh came out closer to a sob. ''Come to think of it, apparently, Lawrence preferred death.''

''Lawrence's death had nothing to do with you.''

Her fingers curled against the wallpaper. ''Let's not go down that path again. Look what happened last time. You'd better be careful. If Russ comes out here and sees you breathing down my chest, he's liable to forget his promise and tell the whole world we're getting married.'' When Worth stepped back, she swept regally past him, haughtily drawing aside the skirt of her dress so that not so much as a thread touched him.

His voice stopped her in the doorway to the ballroom. ''You didn't accept my apology, Red.''

''No, I didn't, did I?''

''One other thing.'' He paused.

She waited, her back to him, poised to flee.

''I accept my share of the blame for what happened.''

She whirled around, infuriated by his incredible interpretation of events. ''Your share? The entire blame belongs to you.''

He wore a determined look. The look of a man bent on doing the honorable thing. ''What I told your father this morning. You have every right to hold me to it.''

''Of course I'm going to hold you to it. Weren't you listening to me?'' Turning on her heel, Elizabeth returned to the ballroom. Murdering Mary Lassiter's only son on her wedding day might somewhat ruin the day for Mary.

Worth watched Elizabeth cross the ballroom to where Hannah sat on the floor with Jamie. Despite her stubborn insistence to the contrary, she obviously had no intention of marrying him. Sipping his champagne, he brooded over why he didn't feel overjoyed at his escape. He didn't have to look far for the answer.

Her father. Russ had been furious when he'd discovered Elizabeth in Worth's bed. He wouldn't exactly jump for joy when he learned she wasn't marrying Worth. Yet another wedge would be driven between Russ and Elizabeth.

Courtesy of Worth. Elizabeth hadn't knocked on his door asking for help with Jamie. She hadn't asked him to carry her to his bed.

There was no escaping his responsibility. Beau had spent his life running away from responsibility, but Worth wasn't Beau.

From the moment Elizabeth had rejected his help in the Denver airport, he'd played games with her. Forced her to play along. According to his rules. Because she irritated him.

Across the ballroom, Jamie sat on his mother's hip and chewed the top of her shoulder. Elizabeth's light green dress with pink and white flowers matched St. Chris's ballroom. She might look frail, but she no longer had raccoon eyes from lack of sleep, and temper had lent color to her cheeks.

Watching her, he forced himself to face the truth. He'd deliberately set out to be a thorn in her side. Not to keep her from ruining the wedding. That was a lie he'd told himself to excuse his obnoxious behavior.

The pathetic truth was her rejection of his help had dented his fragile male ego. Even worse, she'd turned his body inside out and didn't have a clue. He'd wanted her, didn't want to want her, and she'd felt nothing for him.

He wondered if, subconsciously, her entire visit he'd been working his way toward something like what happened this morning. To punish her for not wanting to tear off his clothes.

Russ walked up and followed the direction of Worth's gaze. "My grandson needs a father and she needs a husband to take care of her." Russ's cheeks reddened, and he said in a gruff, apologetic voice, "I should have known you wouldn't be sleeping with her if you didn't plan to marry her."

Worth studied the contents of his stemmed glass. Russ's words only reinforced what Worth's conscience had already told him. By his own actions, he'd made himself responsible for Elizabeth and Jamie. He heard Russ ask him when the wedding was. "Elizabeth hasn't said. Don't push her, Russ. I don't think she'll react well to pressure."

"You mean she's darned stubborn. Gets it from her mother. Don't worry. Mary already gave me the dickens for interfering. I'll let you run your courtship the way you want. Just don't take too long over it. It's about time to get that grandson of mine on a horse if we're going to make a cowboy out of him."

Worth looked the older man straight in the eye. "Russ, let's be very clear about one thing. When I marry Elizabeth, Jamie will be my son. His mother and I will decide what he does and when he does it, based on Jamie's wants and needs. I don't care if he's a cowboy or a dishwasher, as long as he's healthy and happy."

Russ stared at him for a long moment before saying flatly, "That's not coming from you. It's from Elizabeth because she thinks I've been a rotten father."

Worth sighed inwardly. The first thing Elizabeth was going to do when they got married was settle things with her father. "It comes from me, Russ. I'm just saying, I'm adopting Jamie, and he'll be my son in every sense of the word."

Mary came up and dragged Russ away to talk to someone. Worth leaned against the wall and sipped champagne.

Elizabeth was bent over, hanging on to Jamie's hands as the little boy tottered unsteadily over to Hannah. His little legs were getting sturdier. He'd soon be walking on his own.

James Lassiter. Worth silently tested the name. And was surprised by how right it sounded. He smiled slightly as Jamie pulled one hand free of Elizabeth's hold and kept toddling toward Hannah.

Worth switched his gaze to Jamie's mother. Her silky dress molded her lovely shape in a way that made him hope she'd let him into her bed before they tied the knot.

They wouldn't have love, but they'd have passion.

A couple of wide-eyed tourists, guide book in hand, peeked into the ballroom, and Worth gestured to them to come in, pointing them toward the champagne. Thomas would have made sure there was plenty to serve the hotel guests and tourists who wandered in off the street. That was the price of having a wedding reception in St. Chris's historic ballroom. The family was used to it. Even Elizabeth was smiling graciously at an uninvited male.

Recognizing that particular male, Worth's tolerance vanished and he straightened fast.

"This must be Lawrence, Jr. He's a fine-looking boy."

Elizabeth's head whipped around at the familiar voice. Professor Burns might be talking about her son, but his eyes went directly to her chest. She quickly lifted Jamie and stood up straight. "His name is James Lawrence. I call him Jamie."

"You look more like your usual self than you did in that rather provocative dress you wore the other night, my dear." Equal parts disapproval and disappointment filled his voice.

Elizabeth clamped her back teeth together.

Her silence failed to register on his self-absorbed ego. He waved a careless hand. "My friends insisted I postpone my leave-taking." A sudden frown creased his head. "Here comes that..." His face cleared. "Give him your child, so we can take advantage of this lovely music, my dear."

Jamie started bouncing excitedly in her arms, chattering at someone behind her. Elizabeth didn't need to look to know who stood there.

Worth took Jamie from her. "Hey, Gus, what's happening?"

Augustine Burns gave him an imperial nod before turning to Elizabeth. "I believe this is my dance, my dear."

Elizabeth plastered her hand across Worth's mouth as he opened it. "I'll handle this." She turned to the professor. "I am not your dear, Professor Burns, and I will never be your dear."

"My d—that is, Elizabeth, I apologize if you think I'm being overly familiar. I'm merely trying to do what Lawrence would want me to do now that he has passed. He wouldn't want you worrying your pretty little head when I am perfectly willing to do what I can to take care of all your little problems. You need a man to lean on with Lawrence gone, and I'm volunteering to be that man."

His condescending remarks rendered her momentarily speechless.

She'd removed her hand from Worth's mouth, and he took advantage of her stunned silence. "Elizabeth does not want or need your help. She has me to lean on and solve her problems." Jamie had fallen asleep in his arms, and Worth slid his free hand possessively over her hips and then he actually had the audacity to squeeze her bottom.

She knew exactly what he was doing. Because he didn't think she was capable of handling Professor Burns, Worth Lassiter once again had jumped on his white horse and galloped to her rescue. She was sick and tired of being his pet charity.

Augustine Burns' eyes stared in amazement at Worth's hand.

They were both imbeciles.

She started with Augustine Burns. "I'm going to say this just once, Professor Burns. I didn't like you when Lawrence was alive, and I don't like you any better now that he's dead. I'm offended by the way you look at me, and I don't like your sexist, patronizing remarks. If you so much as speak to me again, I'll be forced to complain to the head of your department."

The professor turned bright red and swelled up indignantly. His mouth flapped ineffectually for a second, then he turned on his heel and practically scuttled away.

Worth chuckled.

Elizabeth's wrathful gaze swung around to him. On the brink of telling him to follow the professor right out of her life, she caught herself. Telling him to go away wasn't punishment. What punished Worth Lassiter was the thought of marriage. To her. He deserved to sweat it out a little bit longer.

She pushed away his warm hand and told herself a sudden draft caused the chill on her hip. "When I first came here, remember how you threatened to blackmail me if I didn't do what you wanted me to do?"

His face went very still. "I remember a discussion of some

sort. I wouldn't have said anything to your father. You told me yourself my sisters told you I'm a lousy blackmailer.''

"I, on the other hand, am a very good blackmailer.'' She gave him an icy smile. ''Now that the situation has reversed.'' Playing with his tie, she batted her eyes at him. ''Russ is kind of an old-fashioned daddy and I don't think he'd like it if you backed out of marrying me after having had your way with me, do you?''

"I'm not going to back out.'' His eyes narrowed to slits. ''What are you planning to blackmail me about?''

"Well, it's like this, cowboy. Now that I have you trapped, I don't need to bait the trap anymore.'' With a sudden move, she jammed the knot of his tie up against his throat. ''Keep your nose out of my business and your hands off of me.''

She whirled around and ran smack into Thomas Steele. The amused look on his face suggested he'd heard at least part of their conversation. Knowing there was no way to explain it, Elizabeth fled.

Worth loosened his tie and contemplated causing mayhem at his mother's wedding reception. Squeezing Elizabeth's hip might have been a mistake. She defined the word flounce, he decided, watching her toss her hips in an unmistakable display of temper.

Thomas cleared his throat, drawing Worth's attention. ''You know what I'm reminded of?''

"No, and I don't want to know,'' Worth warned his brother-in-law.

"Something you said to me once.'' Thomas didn't bother to hide the laughter in his eyes. ''You have certainly stepped in it this time.''

"Shut up,'' Worth snarled. He was halfway across the ball-room before he realized Jamie still slept in his arms. Judging by the angry, defensive look on Jamie's mother's face as she zoomed back across the room, Worth wasn't the only one who'd forgotten he held her son.

"Give him to me. I'm taking him up to bed.''

She'd insisted on staying at St. Chris's tonight. More proof that she had no intention of marrying him.

"I'll take him up."

"I can manage on my own," she snapped.

"I need the practice."

"I doubt you need practice doing anything."

He needed practice handling redheads, but he knew he'd get plenty of that during the next fifty years or so of marriage. The feeling of sick disappointment which had accompanied the thought of marriage earlier today seemed to have faded. Proving a man could adjust to anything if he had to.

Glaring at him, Elizabeth waited for him to hand Jamie to her. Holding the boy securely, he headed out of the ballroom.

She caught up with him at the elevator. "If you think I'm going to let you start in where you left off this morning, you have another think coming."

He couldn't help teasing her. "Ah, now I see why you think I don't need any practice. You did give the impression that you were happy with my performance this morning."

Her cheeks immediately lit up with a fiery blush. "That is not what I meant. I meant you are so arrogant that you don't think you need to practice anything."

"That's where you're wrong." He pushed the button to call the elevator. "I need to practice putting my son to bed."

If he'd questioned her intentions before, the white, stricken look on Elizabeth's face told the truth. More than anything, she regretted Jamie had no father. She'd just realized that by refusing to marry Worth, she was depriving her son of a father.

Worth jabbed the elevator button again. "And then you can practice taking my clothes off."

CHAPTER TEN

ELIZABETH stared fixedly at the inside of the wood-paneled elevator. She knew darned well her cheeks matched the red in the plaid golf slacks worn by the gentleman who'd joined them in time to hear Worth's outrageous remark.

"Cute kid," the man said to Worth. "Seems like only yesterday my son was that age and now he's a doctor."

Elizabeth heard the pride in the man's voice and blocked out the rest of the conversation. It would be easy to accept Worth's sacrifice. And not totally selfish. Not if she married him for Jamie's sake. A boy needed a father. Her knowledge of football barely covered the basics, and she'd never memorized a baseball statistic in her life.

Worth had called Jamie his son.

He'd make a great father. He and Jamie went together like strawberries and shortcake.

She loved strawberries and shortcake.

The elevator stopped and the metal gate folded open. If she tried to wrest Jamie from Worth, he'd just embarrass her again.

Unlocking the door, Elizabeth stood back to let Worth enter. Silently she unpacked a sleeper for Jamie. Her son woke up as Worth changed him, sucked sleepily on his bottle, gave a loud burp as Worth patted his back, and was asleep again before his head touched the sheets in the baby bed.

Worth pulled a small blanket over Jamie and followed Elizabeth out to the sitting room of the suite Thomas had insisted on installing her in. Sprawling on the sofa, he undid his suit jacket and unfastened his tie, leaving the ends hanging down his shirt front. Like a man who planned to stay awhile.

"Don't get comfortable. You're not staying," Elizabeth said.

"We need to talk." He patted the sofa beside him.

She didn't want to talk. She knew what he was going to say. He was going to be boringly self-sacrificing. Offer himself on the altar of marriage. Because he blamed himself.

It had to be said. "If I hadn't been such a crybaby last night, it would never have happened." She sat stiffly on the edge of an upholstered wingback chair across from him.

"You didn't cry."

"You know what I mean. If I hadn't said anything, you wouldn't have felt sorry for me. You would have slept alone in your bed and I would have slept alone in mine."

"It wouldn't have been nearly as much fun." Worth smiled, a sexy curve of his lips which jumbled her insides and set aflame the nerve endings beneath her skin.

And conjured up memories of his pleasure-giving mouth and fingers. Pleasure her body remembered all too well.

Her eyes shot to his and the gentle compassion she saw there humiliated her. Dredging up anger, she asked acidly, "Fun for whom? You never removed your jeans. Unless you get your kicks out of proving you have some kind of power and control over women."

"Elizabeth, that isn't—"

"Forget it. It doesn't matter. Call it widow's itch." Looking him straight in the eye, she brought out the lie. "Any man who touched me would have evoked the same response." She dared him to call her a liar.

"I'm better prepared now."

"Good for you. Why don't you hurry down to the reception before everyone leaves and see if you can find another pitiful woman and administer a dose of charitable sex to her?"

Worth unbuttoned the collar of his white shirt. "I knew you'd have a temper."

"You're too good to be true," she marveled, using anger to fight the pain. "I'm afraid of horses, I have a temper, I'm puny, I'm pitiful, you hate the way I wear my hair, and still, you're willing to sacrifice your dreams to marry me." A blind man couldn't have missed the way he winced at the word marry.

Or the way he squared his shoulders and firmed his jaw with resolve. Prepared to swallow the bitter pill. ''I'll bet everyone in Aspen calls you St. Worth.''

''Maybe I should have said something this morning when—'' He bit off the rest of the sentence.

Elizabeth finished it for him. ''When I first seduced you. Go ahead and say it. I know what I did. The problem wasn't what I did. It was your interpretation. I thought I was suggesting mutual pleasure. You thought I was begging to be taken care of.''

He gave her a thoughtful look. ''Suppose I begged you to take care of me? How many times would call us even?''

''When it comes to charity, I already gave at the office,'' she said in a caustic voice.

Shrugging out of his jacket, Worth laid it across the back of the sofa. ''I think we'd accomplish more if we changed the subject from sex, and talked about marriage instead.''

''No.''

''I want to marry you, Elizabeth. Do you at least believe that?''

She believed it. Unfortunately, he wanted to marry her for all the wrong reasons. ''I don't want to marry you.''

''Russ would be pleased.''

''I'm not in the habit of marrying to please my father.''

Taking off his tie, Worth carefully folded and refolded it, before giving her a level look. ''If you are concerned about what kind of father I'd make to another man's son, I promise you I will be the best father to Jamie that I can. I will love him as much as I will love the rest of our children.''

Elizabeth inhaled sharply. Worth didn't need to tell her that. He had a generous, loving heart as big as all outdoors. That was why she loved him. Her anger collapsed like a pricked balloon.

Her love for Lawrence had been immature and superficial. They'd never shared their fears and aspirations. Two cardboard people in a cardboard marriage. She'd never questioned her lack of interest in seeing beyond Lawrence's surface to explore his inner self.

After two weeks she knew more about Worth than she'd learned about Lawrence in a year of marriage.

Her throat swelled with unshed tears. There were so many things she'd never learn about Worth. She wanted to peel him like an onion, learn his secrets, peer into his soul.

She'd been in love with Lawrence and wanted and expected him to make her happy.

Loving Worth showed her the depth and complexities of genuine love. She wanted him, but loving him, she had to let him go. Being in love, one took. Loving, one gave. The most loving thing she could give Worth was his freedom.

She wanted to be his love, not his responsibility.

The pain began to eat through her rigid control. If she hadn't come to Aspen... No. The one thing she refused to regret was coming here, meeting Worth.

Adversity could defeat you or make you strong. She wasn't strong yet, but she would be. She had Jamie. She'd survive.

Crossing the floor, Elizabeth sank to her knees in front of Worth and took his hands in hers. "Worth, you will make a wonderful father. I wish Jamie could be your son, but he can't be."

"He could be."

She shook her head. "I can't marry you just so I'll have a husband and Jamie will have a father. I can't marry you to please Russ or your mother or anyone else. I can't marry you because you feel sorry for me and feel responsible for what happened. You're not responsible for me or for Jamie. I'm responsible for me and for my son. I thank you for the offer, but I cannot and will not take you up on it."

Worth tightened his fingers around hers. His gaze never left her face. "We could make it work, Red."

"One man already married me for the wrong reasons. I won't let another man do the same. I want you to have your adventures. Travel. Be footloose and fancy free. One day, when you're ready to settle down, you'll find a woman to love and you'll have children of your own to love.''

''I want to love your child.''

He said nothing about wanting to love her. She wanted him to lie, but if he lied, he wouldn't be the man she loved.

Elizabeth lifted his hands to her lips and pressed a kiss on each. ''Thank you,'' she said. ''Thank you for your many kindnesses to Jamie and thank you for being willing to marry me. Thank you for entertaining me and thank you for last night and this morning.'' Ignoring the heat coloring her cheeks, she let her eyes roam over every inch of his face, imprinting it on her brain. Later she would be able to recall every tiny wrinkle, every pore. The exact shade of blue.

The blue darkened and he said her name impatiently.

She laid a finger against his lips. ''Most of all, thank you for forcing me to remember who and what I am.''

Tugging his face close to hers, she kissed him fiercely. When he would have made more of the kiss, she pulled away, sitting on her heels, her back held rigidly straight. ''You'd better go now.''

Worth stood and looked down at her. ''You sleep on your decision. We'll talk in the morning.''

Elizabeth folded her hands together. A person had only so much willpower. She summoned up the last of hers. ''No. This is goodbye. The hotel van is taking me to the airport. I've already made arrangements.''

He started to say something, changed his mind, and walked slowly out the door.

Out of her life.

Pride and courage abandoned her and she slumped back on her heels, staring at the bloodless fingers clenched together in her lap. She'd done the right thing. She ought to be feel noble and virtuous and good.

If a herd of horses had pounded her insides into pulp, she couldn't feel more bruised and battered. Slumping over on the carpet, Elizabeth curled into a fetal position and repeated over and over again that she would make it. She and Jamie would be okay. They would be. They would.

Tears leaked from her eyes. It wasn't fair that doing the wrong thing seemed so right while doing the right thing caused such pain.

Enough makeup could hide anything. Clutching the edge of the cold marble countertop, Elizabeth studied her face in the mirror and hoped she'd camouflaged red-rimmed eyes. Giving in to tears the night before had been a mistake. All her weaknesses, her frailties, her emotions had washed to the surface.

Pressing her palms flat against the hard marble, she forced herself to breathe slowly and deeply. In the bedroom Jamie bounced in the crib and jabbered. Think of him. Breathe slowly. In and out.

A sharp knock on the door of the suite heralded the arrival of the bellman, come for her luggage. Picking up Jamie, she looked around one last time. Professionally, Elizabeth approved of the well-appointed, beautifully decorated suite. Personally, she didn't care if she ever again saw vine-patterned carpeting or Art Nouveau furniture.

Jamie practically leaped from her arms when Elizabeth opened the door. She inhaled sharply. "I told you I have a ride to the airport."

Worth indicated her luggage to the bellman, canceled the van at the front desk, and drove her to Aspen airport. She made no further protest because if she opened her mouth, the wrong words might come rushing out. She'd made her decision. The right decision. Living with tears and pain would be easier than living with a man who felt nothing for her but responsibility.

He sat beside her on the commuter plane to Denver. She looked out the window. He played with Jamie. At Denver airport they both directed their words to Jamie.

Elizabeth grew tense as the time of her departure neared. She fumbled for the words to send him away before she weakly gave in. "Thank you. We'll be fine from here. You don't need to wait."

"I'll wait."

She tried to pretend it didn't matter. "I talked to Mary and Russ briefly this morning before they left for Vancouver. I didn't say anything about us. I'll write them a letter while they're gone."

"Elizabeth—"

Interrupting him, she plowed ahead. "Have you decided where you'll go first? What you'll do?"

After a minute, he said, "I suppose China. I've always wanted…"

When he didn't finish, she said determinedly, "I'm sure you'll love it. Different food, interesting culture, beautiful sights."

A disembodied voice announced advance boarding for her flight, and thankfully, Elizabeth stood, reaching for Jamie. "I guess this is goodbye. Thank you again, and have fun on your travels."

Worth carried Jamie and her largest bag on the plane. Before handing her son to her, Worth gave him a big hug and kiss. "You be a good boy and take care of your mom, Jimbo."

Elizabeth swallowed hard. "Jamie," she said for the last time.

"Have a good flight, Red."

"We will."

"I'll send you a postcard from China."

"No," she said sharply. "Don't."

His intense gaze thoroughly scrutinized her face before he said, "All right." Bending down he gave her a hard, swift kiss, and then he was gone, striding down the aisle, a tall man in a black cowboy hat. Walking out of her life.

Because she'd sent him away.

Elizabeth stared blindly at the upright seat back in front of her. Boarding passengers banged into her shoulder, but she was numb to physical sensation.

Suddenly Jamie bounced excitedly on her lap. "Wa, Wa, Wa!" he cried, clapping his hands with glee.

For a split second Elizabeth allowed herself to hope, looking up at the tall cowboy sitting down across the aisle.

"Sorry, ma'am. Didn't mean to bump you." The man placed his black, wide-brimmed hat on his knee and smoothed his silver hair.

Jamie shrank back in his mother's arms and thrust his thumb in his mouth. He stared at Elizabeth with big blue eyes and didn't make a sound as warm drops of water fell on his face.

Worth reined in Wally and pulled off his slicker, rolling it up and securing it behind the saddle. The pungent odors of wet earth and damp pine filled his nostrils. As a small boy, he'd ridden with his grandfather Yancy after summer rain squalls. Yancy had taught him how to see. One day Worth would do the same for his sons and daughters and grandchildren, pointing out the dainty deer tracks in the muddy trail or the flash of yellow as a small warbler darted between branches in a patch of willows.

Mist rose from the grass, blurring the green grass.

Forcibly reminding him of Elizabeth's green, tear-smeared eyes as he'd walked away from her.

He'd always hated saying goodbye at airports. Hated seeing everyone else's excitement and anticipation while he stayed behind. His lingering depression since she'd left was nothing more than impatience to start his adventures.

The old man at the airport had talked about adventures. Standing beside Worth at the large window, he beamed at him. "Seeing the wife and kid off to Grandma and Grandpa?" The man hadn't waited for an answer. "Good-looking family."

It had been easier to thank the man than explain.

"I wish I was your age again, starting out on the big adventure. Getting to know a woman. Raising a family. Never knowing what tomorrow is going to bring, but jumping out of bed each morning eager to face the day. Because each day is something new, something exciting, married to the right woman. I envy you, young man." The man didn't seem to notice the moisture filling his faded eyes. "My Ella's been dead five years now, but what an adventure we had."

Wally stamped an impatient foot, and Worth nudged the stallion into an easy lope. The old man missed his wife, that was all. You couldn't compare hiking the Appalachian Trail to being tied down to a family.

He wondered if Jamie was walking yet.

What would Elizabeth say if he called her to find out?

Another question hit him, and Wally stumbled as Worth unconsciously pulled back too hard on the reins. He patted the stallion's neck. "Sorry, boy."

The unanswered question nagged at him all day. He told himself it would go away when he pulled out the travel brochures. If wasn't as if he'd lost interest in them. He'd been busy.

Sitting at his desk, the question popped up again. What if he called Elizabeth?

What if a man answered her phone?

A month had passed since they'd returned to Nebraska. After reading her letter explaining she and Worth were not getting married, her father had phoned her and they'd had a long talk.

A good talk. Over twenty years of misunderstandings had been cleared up. She'd confessed her fear of horses, and Russ made it clear he didn't care if she ever went near a horse again. She was still his favorite daughter. Elizabeth had kept her secret about Lawrence's betrayal, but they'd talked about his funeral, with both of them shedding a few tears over Russ's apology. The conversation had ended on a note of closer understanding than they'd shared in years.

Sometimes the days she'd spent in Hope Valley seemed like a long-ago movie Elizabeth had seen of someone else's life. Until she saw a certain shade of blue and memories would taunt her with what could have been.

Perhaps someday she'd be able to remember the good times without remembering the pain.

And maybe the night would come when she could fall asleep

without seeing Worth Lassiter in her dreams. Without her body remembering his touch.

It was absolutely the craziest thing he'd ever done. If one of his sisters had contemplated doing something like this before she got married, Worth would have locked her up.

Crazy courtships were normal for Lassiters.

Worth wiped his palms on his jeans. He was betting his future on Elizabeth being as crazy as he was.

An eighteen-wheeler zoomed past, violently rocking the trailer behind him. After a couple of knuckle-whitening moments, Worth had everything under control again.

He didn't expect to have much of anything under control in the future. Not with that red hair.

At first, Elizabeth ignored the honking horn. With a teenager living next door, honking horns were the norm. The horn sounded again, impatient, demanding. Continuous.

The noise was going to wake Jamie from his nap if she didn't put a stop to it. On her way to the front door Elizabeth glanced out of a window. Her heart stopped and her feet froze to the floor.

A dusty, dark-blue pickup with a travel trailer in tow was parked at her curb. A cowboy stood outside the pickup leaning against the side of it. With his wide-brimmed, black hat, jean-clad legs, boots and blue chambray shirt, he looked as if he'd stepped straight out of a Hollywood western.

What was Worth doing here?

For a second, hope reigned, but reality quickly set in. She should have known her father wouldn't give up so easily.

Worth reached through the open truck window and tattooed another summons on the horn.

The blare of noise aroused Elizabeth from her trancelike state, and she dashed outside. Closing the door behind her, she clung to the doorknob. "Stop honking before you wake up Jamie."

A zillion questions hovered on the tip of her tongue. She lacked the nerve to ask even one. His unexpected appearance had caught her with her defenses down. He had no right to drop back into her life.

Greedily she took in every square inch of him. He was the sexiest-looking man she'd ever seen.

Elizabeth reminded herself she'd moved on. Made plans.

Worth Lassiter played no part in those plans.

Pushing his hat to the back of his head, he unleashed his killer smile. "You ever been to Mesa Verde, Red?"

The incongruous question threw her even more off balance. Worth did nothing without a purpose, but what old Indian ruins in Colorado had to do with her, she couldn't imagine. Eyeing him guardedly, she shook her head.

Shoving his hands in his back pockets, Worth braced a shoulder against the truck. "Me, neither. Did you know they think the first people lived in the area about two thousand years ago? The cliff dwellings came later, around 1200 A.D."

"I see." She saw nothing. And then she did. Dropping to the concrete steps, she stared blankly at him. Russ had somehow forced Worth to come after her, no doubt playing heavily on Worth's overdeveloped sense of responsibility. Because Worth was an extremely reluctant suitor, he couldn't bring himself to repeat his offer to marry her. Not that she wanted him to marry her. Not out of pity or duty. "Did Russ send you?" she asked tightly.

He abandoned the pickup and walked up the sidewalk toward her. "He doesn't even know I'm here. He told me he read your letter, said the two of you had had a long talk and patched things up. He never mentioned what happened between us."

Elizabeth didn't want to talk about that. "I thought you'd be standing at the Great Wall of China by now."

"Changed my mind." He sat on the step next to her and stretched out his long legs. "Mesa Verde isn't as old as the Great Wall, but it's a lot closer. We could be there in a couple of days."

"We?" Elizabeth repeated dumbly. He'd come all this way to ask her to go sight-seeing with him? None of this made sense. Her breath caught in her throat. Was this Worth's way of asking her to have an affair with him?

He was nodding. "Pack up Jimbo and your spirit of adventure and let's hit the road."

"Adventure? Hit the road?" She sounded like an idiot, mindlessly echoing him, but her brain refused to function. Drawing up her legs, she hugged them to her chest, compressing herself into a tight, protective huddle. In spite of her defenses, her body quickened. Conscious of his body warmth, his breathing, his scent, she ached to lean into him.

"C'mon, Red, with that hair, you can't convince me you're not an adventurer at heart." His voice wrapped around her, warm and teasing. Seductive.

Elizabeth clenched her hands together, her nails digging into her palms. "I think you'd better tell me exactly why you are here."

"Sometimes a man thinks he has to fly to the moon for adventure and excitement, when the truth is, making love under the moon is a lot more exciting."

Was he saying he'd driven across the state of Nebraska because he wanted to sleep with her? She felt his hand, warm against her neck, his fingers massaging her tight muscles. Closing her eyes, Elizabeth said in a ragged voice, "Stop playing games with me, Worth. I haven't changed my mind since I left Colorado. I am not going to marry you because you feel sorry for me or feel responsible for me or for any other stupid reason like giving Jamie a father."

His fingers went still. "How about because you love me?"

Pain slashed her chest. He didn't play fair. "Nobody said anything about love."

"I'm saying it now. Elizabeth Randall, I love you and want you to marry me."

She didn't believe a word of it. Putting her head on her knees, she mumbled, "Forget it, I don't love you."

Holding her chin, Worth turned her face. "Look at me and say that."

Enigmatic blue eyes told her nothing. Swallowing hard, she said in a commendably firm voice, "I don't love you."

His eyes warmed, the corners crinkling. "I've never met a worse liar in my entire life."

Elizabeth batted his hand away. "It doesn't matter. I am not going to marry you. You might think it kind of you to pretend you love me and want to marry me, but it's not kind, and I refuse to marry you. I will not tie you down. I don't want a restless husband. I want you to be footloose and fancy free. I want you to have your adventures."

"Good, so do I."

She stared hard at his pickup, concentrating on keeping tears from her eyes. "Jamie should be up from his nap soon, if you want to see him before you go."

"Before we go."

Jerking her head around, she said, "Were you listening to me?"

He leaned back on the step, resting his elbows on the top of the concrete stoop. "You said you wanted me to have my adventures. Visiting the Great Wall, now that's a small adventure. A wise man recently told me about the biggest adventure of all, and that's the one I want to go on."

Elizabeth kept her chin up. "What adventure is that?"

"Life. Love. Marriage. Raising a family."

"I knew Russ made you come," she said bleakly.

Reaching up, Worth ran a thumb over her trembling lower lip. "Forget Russ. Forget my mother, my sisters. Forget Lawrence. This is about you and me, Red. Taking on life. Together. What could be more adventurous? Watching Jamie grow up. Having more babies. If that's not adventurous enough for you, we'll make our own adventures. Pack up the family and take off where the spirit of adventure leads us."

His eyes fixed on her face, he took one of her hands in his. "For the longest time, Red, I thought a man had to be alone to have adventures. Maybe some men do, but not me. Without you, there is no adventure.''

She looked helplessly at him. He sounded so sincere, so believable. Elizabeth wanted badly to believe him. How could she when she knew how much he'd fought being tied down? "I can't marry—" A hand over her mouth silenced her.

"Do you love me? Nod yes or shake your head no."

Indecision paralyzed her. If she nodded, he'd continue to lie out of pity, but her muscles refused to let her deny her love.

One corner of his mouth turned up in a sexy little grin and he moved his hand. "Okay, then, let's head 'em up and roll 'em out. What do we do first?"

"I didn't say anything. We don't do anything first."

"I think we do. This." In one move, he hauled her onto his lap and framed her face between his hands. "There's been something missing from my life for so long. Now I know what it is. You. Not pallid adventures like hiking or lying on beaches, but having you in my life. I love you, Red. I plan to spend the rest of my life loving you. Sometimes we'll drive each other crazy, but we'll get over it and move on to more adventures.''

Elizabeth clutched his shoulders. "I didn't say I'd marry you," she said breathlessly.

"You will by the time we reach the first county courthouse in Colorado."

"County courthouse?"

"If you want a big wedding with all the trimmings, that's okay, but I'm not waiting until then to sleep with you. I'll wait until the first courthouse, but that's my limit."

"You don't have to wait—"

"Good."

She'd meant because she wasn't going to marry him, but the way he kissed her drove every coherent thought, every objection out of her mind. By the time he raised his head, she would have agreed to anything he suggested. As she cuddled against his broad chest, the trailer caught her eye. "Why the trailer?"

"Adventure, Red. Jimbo's going to love it. I built in a crib for him."

"Jamie."

Giving her a loving smile, he shook his head. "You're his mother and you can call him what you want, but I'm calling him Jimbo until he tells me different. No, Red, wait." Alarm filled his voice. "If it really upsets you, I'll call him Jamie."

She shook her head and wiped her eyes. "I'm not marrying you for Jamie's sake. You do know that."

He gave her a wicked grin. "You're marrying me to get my jeans off."

"If you don't quit smiling at me like that," she said in a shaky voice, "I'm going to rip them off you right out here on my front steps."

Laughing, he lifted her to her feet and stood. "That may be a little too much adventure even for me."

Worth lay stretched out on the bed, the sheet pulled up to his waist gleaming white against his tanned chest. His arms were folded beneath his head, his eyes closed. Deliberately putting off the moment until she'd join him, Elizabeth stood in the doorway, watching him.

They'd been married two weeks. Two weeks of love and laughter and learning about each other. From the bottoms of his bare feet to the top of his brown hair, she loved every inch of him. "Glad to be back in your own bed?" she asked.

"I will be." He opened his eyes and turned his head to smile at her.

The sensual look in his eyes left no doubt as to his meaning. And caused meltdown in her bones. She returned his smile. "Have I told you how much I love adventuring with you?"

Satisfaction covered his face. "Have I ever told you how much I approve of those green pajamas?"

He'd never asked where she'd gotten them, but he must wonder. "My mother gave them to me last Christmas." She hesitated. "Lawrence hated me in green. He said a redhead wearing green was a cliché."

Worth cocked his head, running his eyes possessively over her. "You know, Red, as much as I hate the idea I could ever think like Lawrence about anything, I find myself agreeing with him," he said in a serious voice. "Those green pajamas are all wrong for you." He waited a heartbeat. "Take them off, Red."

She saw the loving laughter in his eyes. He didn't think she'd do it.

Slowly she unbuttoned the top button of her pajamas. Worth quit laughing about the fourth button. The next button gave her an exorbitant amount of trouble. She loved the way his breathing quickened.

"Jimbo can unbutton faster than you can," he said in a thickened voice.

Giving him an artless smile, she slowly pulled open the pajama top and allowed it to slide off her shoulders and down her arms to drop on the floor. Her hair was practically standing on end from all the zinging going on in the bedroom. Hooking her thumbs in the waistband of the bottoms, she gave him what she hoped was a sultry look. "Hey, cowboy, wanna be adventurous?"

In one quick, easy movement, Worth rose from the bed and scooped her up in his arms.

She laughed into his mouth. "I take it that's a yes."

They fell into bed, a warm tangle of arms and legs and loving laughter.

Elizabeth lay curled at his side, her bare bottom resting warmly against his hip. Touching him. Tied to him by marriage. He didn't feel tied down. Or restless. He felt satisfied. Content. Happy. Worth immediately rejected the words as inadequate.

Elizabeth had shown him the true meaning of heartstrings. Not chains binding you down, but ribbons tied around packages of love and wonder. Living with Elizabeth and Jamie was one present after another, each waiting to be opened and cherished. A child's hugs, a woman's smile. Waking up to red hair on his pillow, a hip warm against him. Exploring her mind, her body, her soul took him places he'd never imagined existed.

Beside him, Elizabeth's breathing changed. He sensed her wakening.

"Can't sleep?" she asked drowsily.

"Just thinking."

She went very still. "Having second thoughts?"

He ran his hand over her bottom, welcoming any excuse to touch her. "Never. Just something I've been wanting to talk to you about." He hesitated, unsure how she'd react when he told her he wanted to adopt Jamie. "I intend to be Jimbo's father in every way that matters."

"I know." She rubbed against him like a cat. "I think you ought to adopt him legally. Change his name to James Randall Lassiter. I talked it over with my stepfather, and he agrees."

Hugging her tightly against him, Worth rested a cheek against her hair. "We're going to have a good life." He cupped her belly in time to feel her small quiver of laughter.

Elizabeth lifted his hand and pressed a kiss against his palm. "Good, as in steak?" she asked, amusement running through her voice. She put his hand down on her breast.

Dawn beckoned through the open window. Dawn was the best time of the day. To listen to the birds. To smell the air.

To make love to his wife.

Each day an adventure to be lived. Together.

EPILOGUE

The Double Nickel ranch house sparkled with a fresh coat of white paint in the late afternoon sunshine. The color of the paint on the front door matched the color of the blue flax Elizabeth had planted in lush abundance in front of their home.

Worth looked across the yard as voices came from the renovated guest house. His mother was giving her daughters and their husbands a formal tour of her new home. Mary and Russ had fled to Texas while Elizabeth oversaw construction of the extension to the small cabin, but today Elizabeth and he were throwing a combination housewarming and first wedding anniversary party for their parents.

The tour ended, and Cheyenne and Thomas emerged from the house first, followed by Allie and Zane and Greeley and Quint. Watching the love and laughter surrounding them, satisfaction filled Worth. His sisters had found the mates right for them.

Mary Lassiter Underwood lingered on her porch watching her children and grandchildren. Even from a distance Worth could see the pride on his mother's face, the moisture glinting in her eyes. Happy tears. Mary laid her head on Russ's shoulder as his arm encircled her waist. Worth silently chuckled. One of these days Russ was going to really let go and actually kiss his wife in public.

Children's laughter drew his attention to the patch of lawn beneath the old cottonwood tree. Hannah had insisted there had to be games at a party, and she and Davy and Elizabeth were playing Ring Around the Rosie with the three toddlers. Worth watched the circle of players fall giggling to the ground. Jimbo popped up first and saw Worth watching. Throwing his arms wide, his two-year-old son tore across the yard on skinny little legs, yelling, "Daddy, Daddy."

Worth grabbed him and swung him into the air. "Slow down, Jimbo, the grill's hot."

"Are you fixing hot dogs, Uncle Worth?" Davy and Hannah ran up, twenty-one-month-old Virginia Steele and eighteen-month-old Harmony Peters struggling to keep up with their older siblings. Their fathers came to the little girls' rescue, throwing them up on their shoulders as the whole family gathered around Worth and the barbecue grill.

"You didn't mention you were planning to barbecue," Cheyenne said uneasily.

Elizabeth, her arm linked with Russ's, pealed with laughter. "You're safe. Worth's just supervising heating the grill. I promise not to let him cook anything. Even Jimbo won't eat the charcoal hot dogs his daddy fixes. Worth is the worst cook I've ever known."

Shocked silence met her words.

"He's not that bad," Cheyenne said finally. There wasn't an ounce of conviction in her voice. Her sisters rushed to agree with her. There was no more conviction in their voices.

"Really," Elizabeth said severely, "it's appalling the way you three coddle your brother. He's strong enough to live with the fact that he can't do everything perfectly."

His wife slanted an amused glance his way. Worth knew exactly what she was thinking. His green-eyed redhead thought he did one thing perfectly. She'd told him so this morning as they lay bonelessly content in their bed.

Standing at the head of the table, Worth looked around at his family. Deep satisfaction filled every part of his body. This was what life was all about.

Elizabeth had served champagne with the fancy decorated cake, and he lifted his glass to propose a toast to Mary and Russ.

Everyone at the table followed with their toasts to the happy couple, then Elizabeth stood. "I'd like to make another toast.

The first day I came here, Worth told me about Anna Nichols. Now every time I pass through the ranch gate, I think about how strong she must have been and pray I can live up to her standards. Not that I'll ever ride Wally, mind you, but Rosie and I are getting to be pretty good pals.''

Elizabeth waited until the laughter died down.

''Anna's not here in person, but I'd like to believe she's looking down on us and thinking she started something really fine and wonderful.'' Elizabeth raised her champagne flute. ''To Anna Nichols of Hope Valley. May we always believe, as Anna did, that our futures are filled with hope.'' Looking directly at Worth, she added softly, ''And love and adventure.''

Worth saluted his wife with his glass. He'd hidden the green negligee under the seat in the pickup, planning to present it to Elizabeth next month on their anniversary, but maybe he'd give it to her tonight. He could always buy her another anniversary present.

Neither would come close to equaling the gifts she gave him.

Each wrapped with love.

And tied with heartstrings.

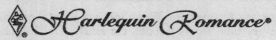
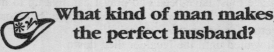

If you enjoyed what you just read,
then we've got an offer you can't resist!

Take 2 bestselling love stories FREE!

Plus get a FREE surprise gift!

Clip this page and mail it to Harlequin Reader Service®

IN U.S.A.
3010 Walden Ave.
P.O. Box 1867
Buffalo, N.Y. 14240-1867

IN CANADA
P.O. Box 609
Fort Erie, Ontario
L2A 5X3

YES! Please send me 2 free Harlequin Romance® novels and my free surprise gift. Then send me 4 brand-new novels every month, which I will receive months before they're available in stores. In the U.S.A., bill me at the bargain price of $2.90 plus 25¢ delivery per book and applicable sales tax, if any*. In Canada, bill me at the bargain price of $3.34 plus 25¢ delivery per book and applicable taxes**. That's the complete price and a savings of over 10% off the cover prices—what a great deal! I understand that accepting the 2 free books and gift places me under no obligation ever to buy any books. I can always return a shipment and cancel at any time. Even if I never buy another book from Harlequin, the 2 free books and gift are mine to keep forever. So why not take us up on our invitation. You'll be glad you did!

116 HEN CNEP
316 HEN CNEQ

Name	(PLEASE PRINT)	
Address	Apt.#	
City	State/Prov.	Zip/Postal Code

* Terms and prices subject to change without notice. Sales tax applicable in N.Y.
** Canadian residents will be charged applicable provincial taxes and GST.
All orders subject to approval. Offer limited to one per household.
® are registered trademarks of Harlequin Enterprises Limited.

HROM99   ©1998 Harlequin Enterprises Limited

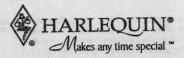